'I want to ki

'Do you think tha

'Probably not.' He edged nearer with agonising slowness. Claire wasn't sure what to do. All she knew for certain was that he was evoking emotions in her she'd never felt before. He seemed to understand her, better than anyone else she'd ever met. It was uncanny, surreal—but also such a relief. 'Do you want me to kiss you?' he murmured, his body almost pressing against her, the heat radiating out.

'Umm...yeah.' He was so close, so wildly masculine, and she definitely craved a taste.

Declan smiled. 'Is that the answer or just a mumble?' He breathed in deeply, her intoxicating scent winding its way about him once more.

Claire couldn't wait any longer, her fingers reaching out to tentatively touch his warm chest. Closing her eyes, she marvelled at the sensation, and felt a shudder course over her spine.

Finally. Declan pressed his lips to hers and she sighed into the kiss. This was good. This was nice. This was right.

Lucy Clark began writing romance in her early teens, and immediately knew she'd found her 'calling' in life. After working as a secretary in a busy teaching hospital, she turned her hand to writing medical romance. She currently lives in South Australia with her husband and two children. Lucy largely credits her writing success to the support of her husband, family and friends.

Recent titles by the same author:

A KNIGHT TO HOLD ON TO
CHRISTMAS DAY FIANCÉE*
CRISIS AT KATOOMBA HOSPITAL*
DR CUSACK'S SECRET SON

Blue Mountains A&E

IN HIS
SPECIAL CARE

BY
LUCY CLARK

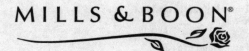

MILLS & BOON®

First published in Great Britain 2006
Harlequin Mills & Boon Limited,
Eton House, 18-24 Paradise Road, Richmond, Surrey TW9 1SR

© Lucy Clark 2006

Standard ISBN 0 263 84751 9
Promotional ISBN 0 263 85140 0

Set in Times Roman 10 on 11 pt
03-0806-58235

Printed and bound in Spain
by Litografia Rosés, S.A., Barcelona

IN HIS
SPECIAL CARE

For Tina, best school principal.
Many thanks for sharing your special gifts.
Ps 112

CHAPTER ONE

'Is HE here yet?'

'Yes. He's already on his third patient. Claire, where have you been?' Bethany, the clinic nurse, put down the telephone receiver as Claire walked through the door. 'I've been calling your cell phone for the past half-hour.'

'I know, I know. I'm sorry. It was at the bottom of my bag and I couldn't stop to get it out while I was driving.'

'What's happened? Is anything wrong?'

'Nothing major. I had a bad night with Brett.' Claire Neilson dumped her bag and car keys with the nurse, knowing she'd lock them away.

'Again?' There was concern in Bethany's tone. 'Is he all right?'

'He's fine. Under control...I think. Teenagers! Who'd have them?' Claire quickly donned a white coat and searched around for her stethoscope. 'Where is it?' She was starting to stress.

'Here.' Bethany handed her the instrument. 'Go. He's in clinic room two and he's not happy.'

'Great,' Claire mumbled. 'Just what I don't need.' She didn't pause or knock before entering the room. This was her hospital with her patients and she was used to barrelling through any problem which came her way. Today's problem was called Declan Silvermark, the new otorhinolaryngologist taking up a specialist rotation at Mt Black Hospital.

Mt Black may not have been big by normal town standards but the population had increased dramatically over the last two decades to make it stand out on the map. It had two high schools, one university, three swimming pools, two tennis courts and a golf club. Situated three hours inland from Brisbane, it had been an old mining town in the nineteenth century but the gold had long since dried up. The population hadn't.

Claire walked into the room to find Mrs Cameron sitting on the examination bed beside her four-year-old son Pierce, her hands clamped around his shoulders as she tried to get him to sit still. Pierce had his eyes screwed up tight and was kicking his legs in the air.

Standing in front of the bed, but not too close, was a man with dark brown hair and blue eyes. He was dressed in covered shoes, navy trousers and wore a white medical coat buttoned precisely all the way up. She could just see the top of his shirt and perfectly knotted tie above the wide collar of the coat. Pristine, perfect and pompous. Those were the first words that came to mind to describe Declan Silvermark. He was also squeaky-clean handsome, definitely not her type at all—not that she was looking for any romantic entanglements. Quite the opposite, in fact. Claire was looking forward to peace, quiet and solitude. Heaven knew, she'd earned it.

The new ENT looked to be in his mid-twenties but she knew that wasn't possible, not with the specialist training he'd have completed. He'd need to be at least in his mid-thirties. Not that she was a young spring chicken herself. She'd be thirty next birthday although some days, such as today, she felt a lot older. She supposed that's what happened when responsibility was thrust upon a person at an early age.

'Oh, Claire.' Eileen Cameron looked at her gratefully. 'There you are. Pierce has decided to be uncooperative this morning.'

Claire briefly made eye contact with Dr Silvermark but didn't say a word. She wasn't in the mood for polite chit-chat or introductions. She was in the mood to get the already delayed clinic organised and completed as soon as possible. That didn't mean, however, she intended to rush her patients.

She walked over to Pierce, stepping in front of Dr Silvermark. 'Excuse me,' she said softly, and could feel his disapproving eyes glaring daggers into her back. She didn't care. Settling Pierce down was her first priority, otherwise they'd get nowhere.

'Pierce?' She held up her hand, making sure she avoided his kicking legs. 'Pierce? Pierce?'

She waited until he met her gaze, then smiled. 'How's it going?' she greeted him cheerfully. 'Give me five, buddy.'

The boy stopped kicking for a split second, gave Claire a wide grin and slapped her hand before wriggling again. 'I don't *want* to sit still.'

Claire picked him up off the examination couch and set him on the floor. 'You don't have to, sweetheart.' Again, Claire could feel Dr Silvermark's glare. She glanced up briefly, noting the frown on the man's face, which made him look a little older...but not much.

'Yay.' Pierce began running around the small clinic room in circles pretending he was riding a horse.

'Of course,' Claire continued, 'you won't get any jelly beans when you leave.'

Pierce stopped, regarded her closely for a minute before returning to his running. Claire walked over to her sweet jar and gave it a shake. 'Ooh. Look at all the red ones. Red ones are my favourite. Are they your favourite, Eileen?'

'Oh, yes. The red ones are delicious.'

'No!' Pierce stopped running and stamped his foot. 'I like the red ones best. You can't eat them.'

'I can if I've been good.' Claire gave the jar another rattle before setting it in the middle of the shelf where the four year old could quite clearly see it, even though it was still out of his reach. It was bribery at its best, but with Pierce it worked every time, and as she'd learned many years ago it was always best to go with what worked...within reason.

'What about him?' Pierce pointed to Dr Silvermark, who was now standing to the side of the room, broad arms crossed firmly over his chest, watching the event with cool indifference. Claire was mildly disappointed. She'd hoped this ENT specialist was going to be better than the last. Dr Bean had looked down his nose at her, the hospital and the patients in it from the moment he'd arrived. When he'd handed in his forced resignation to the hospital board, Claire had been relieved as well as happy. 'Is he gonna eat my red ones?'

'I don't know,' Claire answered the boy truthfully. 'Why don't you ask him?'

'Hey, Mr Doctor,' Pierce said sternly. 'You like the red ones? 'Cause you can't have any 'cause they're for me, 'cause I been good.'

'No, you haven't,' his mother contradicted, but Pierce continued to stare at Dr Silvermark.

Claire watched as, for the first time since she'd walked into the room, the man smiled. The instant he did, she felt her knees weaken. Dr Silvermark's entire face changed. His blue eyes twinkled, his lips curved up. Wow! Now he was Dr Dreamy instead of Dr Dreary. Not that she was looking to dream about him. Well…dreaming couldn't hurt, could it? She shook her head and cleared her silly thoughts.

'Actually, I like white ones,' Dr Silvermark answered. Claire couldn't stop the tingles that flooded her body at his smooth, deep voice. Mmm, *very* dreamy. She'd always been a sucker for a deep voice. Deep voice and nice eyes. Those were the things she liked in a man…as well as the usual—honesty, compassion, understanding. The basics.

'Good.' Satisfied, Pierce turned to his mother. 'And no red ones for you today, Mummy, and none for you, Dr Claire.'

'Well…' Claire pulled herself together, deciding Dr Silvermark could keep his mouth shut so she could concentrate on her job, rather than on his delicious voice. She crouched down to look at Pierce. Here was another heartbreaker in the making. His big brown eyes could melt the hardest of hearts and right now Pierce was in 'determination' mode. Good. Perhaps now she'd get some co-operation from him. She reached out and took his chin gently in her hand, ensuring their eyes met. 'You know the rules, Pierce. You sit still, you get a reward. You run around, no reward. Your choice.' She held his gaze for a moment longer before dropping her hand back to her side.

'Hmm.' Pierce put his head on the side and regarded her thoughtfully. Claire tried not to laugh out loud at his gorgeousness. 'OK' he said after a moment of reflection, his voice almost annoyed at having to give in. 'I sit still.'

'Thank you, sweetheart.'

Pierce held out his hands to Claire who dutifully picked him up and placed him back on the examination couch. Again, she angled his chin up so their gazes could meet. 'Now, you promise to sit still for Dr Silvermark?'

'So you do know who I am,' came the quiet comment from behind her. 'Interesting.'

'I promise,' Pierce said solemnly.

'Excellent.'

'And then I get the red jelly beans?'

'Yes.' Claire stepped aside, allowing Dr Silvermark access to little Pierce, wondering whether she'd really heard him make that comment. Instead, she focused on taking two red sweets from the jar and placing them on a tissue in plain view of Pierce. 'Just keep your eye on the prize and all will be fine,' she said, but realised her words were too late as Pierce was already doing just that. 'Ah, incentive,' she said as Dr Silvermark picked up the otoscope. 'Works like a charm.'

She was pleased to see that Dr Silvermark followed her lead and took Pierce's chin in his hand, ensuring the boy made eye contact with him before speaking. 'All right, then, Pierce. I'm going to shine a light into your ear and have a good look at what's inside, but I need you to sit very still so I can see right into your eardrum,' Dr Silvermark said, before shining the light into Pierce's ear.

Pierce's eyebrows shot upwards. 'I have drums in my head! Is that why Mummy says I'm loud?'

Claire smiled, Eileen chuckled. Dr Silvermark merely concentrated on the task at hand, saying quite calmly, 'It is sort of like a drum. The real name is the tympanic membrane. It's like the skin on a drum and provides an airtight seal. When the sound waves hit it, the tympanic membrane begins to vibrate.'

'Cool. Hey, Mum.' Pierce turned to speak to his mother and Dr Silvermark quickly pulled the instrument clear.

'Sit still, sweetheart,' Claire reminded, pointing to the sweets.

'Oh. Yeah. Forgot.' Fixing his eyes firmly on those sweets, he sat still so Dr Silvermark could reposition the otoscope before checking the other ear. Finally, Dr Silvermark straightened and reached for the casenotes, perusing them for a moment.

'Mrs Cameron. You said that Pierce has been having ear drops.'

'Yes.'

'Morning and night?'

'Yes.' Eileen glanced at Claire. Claire shrugged.

'Two drops in each ear?' he asked.

'Yes. Is something wrong, Doctor?'

Dr Silvermark put the chart down and nodded. 'Actually, there is. Your son has been misdiagnosed and the treatment he's been having for the past…' he checked the chart again '…three weeks has only made the problem worse.'

Claire groaned and placed her hand over her eyes for a moment, shaking her head. He'd done it again. The incompetent Dr Bean had once more prescribed an incorrect treatment for a patient. She'd managed to pick up on two other patients who had been misdiagnosed, and had set them on the right medical plan, but to have this happen in front of the new ENT specialist was just downright embarrassing, not to mention the situation for poor little Pierce and his mother.

Then again, that was the reason he was here. Dr Silvermark had been employed to work at the Mt Black Hospital for one week every month. He would hold clinics, both for paediatrics and adults, as well as operating and doing house calls to patients who either lived too far away to get to the hospital or were too sick. As Claire was the leading general practitioner here, it was her duty to show him around…at least for the first week. Dr Bean had been doing clinics here for six months before she'd strongly requested the hospital board to replace him or they'd be looking at numerous law suits.

Dr Silvermark turned to face Claire and spoke quietly to Pierce. The blond-haired doctor appeared to be very good when dealing with her young patient but she obviously wasn't well trained or she wouldn't have prescribed the current course of treatment for Pierce. He didn't like taking another colleague to task for giving the wrong treatment but it had to be done. It wasn't fair to the patient and it wasn't fair to doctors the world over. One doctor misdiagnosing or mistreating a patient gave the rest of them a bad name. 'Excuse me, Dr…?' Declan paused and waited for her to turn to face him.

'Neilson.' Claire stuck out her hand. 'Claire Neilson.' He shifted the pen out of his hand and took hers briefly, but firmly, in his. The instant they made contact, Claire's gaze flicked up to his and he was mesmerised by the rich, browny-gold colour of her eyes.

For a moment, their gazes held. Something…wild and exciting passed between them but, she rationalised, it could just be static electricity from the carpet. It was a lie but it was one she needed to tell herself. She had no desire, no desire at all, to be attracted to the man in front of her. For one, he was her new colleague and dating colleagues never, ever worked out. For two, he'd done nothing but frown at her from the second she'd walked into the room.

'Declan Silvermark.' He found it difficult to break eye contact with her but after drawing in a quick, steadying breath he withdrew his hand, unsure exactly what had just passed between the two of them. At the moment he wasn't sure he liked this woman, especially if she'd been neglecting her patients. It was a good thing he'd accepted the position as a consulting specialist here because if little Pierce was any indication, the patients were in great need of proper medical attention.

'Do I get my sweets now?' Pierce moaned impatiently.

Both Declan and Claire stepped back and gratefully turned their attention to their little patient.

'Of course, sweetheart.' Claire immediately scooped the sweets up, handing them over to the eager boy.

'Yes!' Pierce put both of the red jelly beans into his mouth and clambered down from the examination bed. Claire watched as he went over to the toys in the room and instantly became absorbed in his own little world.

'Pierce?' Eileen said. 'Pierce? Say thank you to Dr Claire.'

There was no response.

'See?' His mother spread her hands wide. 'One minute he hears and the next it's as though there's no one around him.'

Declan nodded and cleared his throat. He'd picked up the case-notes again and was scanning them while his mind cleared from the fog that Dr Claire Neilson had generated. Now, what had he been thinking about before she'd touched him? That's right, he had been about to take her to task. How could he have forgotten? Big choc-olate-brown eyes, honey-blonde hair pulled back in a simple but alluring ponytail, the scent of fresh wild flowers and the electrify-ing touch of her skin against his. Yes, *that's* how he'd forgotten.

'Dr Neilson.' He fixed her with a firm stare. 'It says in his notes he's been having trouble hearing?'

'That's correct. Eileen brought him to see me about six weeks ago.'

Declan frowned. 'And so you just said it was a build-up of wax and put him on drops.'

Claire stared at him in astonishment. 'No. I sent him off for a hearing test.'

'And the results?'

'Are listed in his notes.' Claire strove for patience. Was he trying to blame her for the misdiagnosis?

'And that came back normal,' Mrs Cameron added. 'Accord-ing to *that*, Pierce's hearing is perfect.'

Declan nodded. 'I see. Well, he doesn't have an excess of wax and the ear drops have actually caused a mild infection by rubbing and irritating the tympanic membrane which, if left un-treated, could cause more problems.'

'So what do we do?' Mrs Cameron glanced at her son who was making truck noises as he pushed one around on the carpet.

'Pierce will need to have a course of antibiotics which should clear things up nicely. Does he have any allergies?'

'No.'

'Good. Ceclor should be fine, then. Has he had it before?' As Declan asked the question, he scanned the most recent notes again but couldn't find any previous mention of it. He studied the previous doctor's signature but it was such an odd squiggle that, like most other doctors', it was impossible to decipher. Dr Neilson should learn to print her name after her scrawl.

'No,' Mrs Cameron answered again.

'Good. I doubt he'll have an adverse reaction to it, although he may experience mild diarrhoea but that's nothing to worry about and will settle down once he's finished the antibiotic course. If he gets pains in his tummy or a rash, stop the treatment and bring him back.'

'What about his hearing, though? You said he'd been misdiagnosed. What's the correct diagnosis, then?'

'Auditory processing difficulties. I'd like to run a few more tests, Mrs Cameron, and arrange for Pierce to see an audiologist.'

'What's that?'

Claire smiled at Eileen. 'An audiologist works more one on one with people who have hearing difficulties or ear-related problems. They use things like audiometers, special computer programs and other testing devices.'

'Do we have one here in Mt Black or do I need to take Pierce to Toowoomba or Brisbane?'

'I can arrange for one to come here,' Claire offered.

'I have a colleague I usually refer people to. I'd prefer it if Pierce saw her—that way I know exactly what sort of an assessment to expect.' Using his own contacts would also be better for Pierce's overall treatment. Dr Neilson might not arrange for a suitable audiologist to assess Pierce and then he'd be back to square one.

'So when will that be?' Eileen asked.

'I'll give Louisa a call and let you know. In fact, it might be a good idea to have her come to the hospital one day during the week I'm consulting here on a regular basis.'

Claire nodded, glad he thought that way. It lifted her opinion of him…just a touch. 'Good. I've been trying to get the hospital to agree to a permanent clinic for an audiologist for quite some time, but Dr Bean said he didn't need one.'

Well, at least she wasn't going to fight him on it, even though he had no idea who Dr Bean was. Perhaps Claire Neilson wasn't as bad as he'd initially thought. Doctors weren't infallible. Everyone made mistakes and maybe Pierce was her one mistake. Maybe he shouldn't judge her so hard or so quickly, but on the flip side of the coin, the next time her misdiagnosis could cost someone their hearing or even their life.

Declan glanced at the clock on the wall and realised they needed to get moving. 'I'll leave you with Dr Neilson, to finish up.' He nodded to Mrs Cameron, then bent down to speak to Pierce. He said the boy's name but received no response. Next, he tapped Pierce lightly on the shoulder. Still no response. Pierce was in his own little world. Declan picked up a car from the toy box and began to push it along the ground towards Pierce's truck.

Pierce acknowledged the car. 'Hello, car. Where are you going?' he asked in the deepest voice he could muster. Declan tried hard not to smile.

'I've got to go and see other people now. I wish I could stick around and play for longer but I can't.' Declan also used a different voice from his own and Claire smiled.

This was a different doctor to the one she'd encountered when she'd first walked into the room and she was glad to see it. He may frown, appear standoffish and speak to her in a mildly condescending manner, but if he was as good with all the patients as he was with Pierce, she'd keep him—professionally speaking, of course. She shook her head again, trying to get her thoughts back to normal. Why did they seem to keep flying off on romantic tangents? Declan Silvermark wasn't even her type. Not that she had a type as such. She didn't. She wasn't even looking, wasn't even in the market. Peace and quiet. That was what she was shopping for.

'OK,' Pierce answered.

'Pierce?' Declan said in his own voice. 'Pierce?'

Pierce didn't look up but acknowledged him. 'Yes?'

'Look at me.'

Pierce slowly raised his gaze and finally met Declan's.

'I need to go and see other patients now. Dr Neilson will tell you all about your new medicine.'

'OK.' Pierce went back to playing. Declan nodded and stood. He wrote in the casenotes, then signed and printed his name before addressing Mrs Cameron.

'I'd like to see Pierce next month in my clinic and by then we'll have the results from the audiologist.'

'All right,' Eileen answered, and with a brief nod Declan Silvermark left the room.

Claire sagged with relief the instant he went.

Eileen frowned. 'Was he blaming you for misdiagnosing Pierce?'

Claire shrugged. 'Looks that way.'

'What do you think is wrong with Pierce?'

'Listening problems, just as Dr Silvermark said.'

'So you agree with him?'

'I do. He's right to send him to an audiologist. That would have been my next move but it was my job to refer you on to the ENT specialist. I'm just so sorry Dr Bean made the wrong diagnosis.' Claire watched Eileen's reaction, wondering if she was going to take it further. Dr Bean had clearly been at fault.

'At least it's been picked up early. Don't worry, Claire. I'm not planning to sue the hospital.'

Claire nodded and smiled, relaxing a little. 'It is within your right but, personally, thank you.'

'I trust you, Claire. You delivered Pierce, for heaven's sake. You'd never let anything bad happen to him.'

'Thank you, Eileen.' She was touched. 'That means a lot.'

'You're well respected here, Claire. You put in a lot of time and effort—more so than the hospital board either praise or pay you for, and we're all very grateful for that. Being the only permanent doctor on staff must be wearing on you as well as all the responsibilities you have at home.'

Claire shrugged, feeling self-conscious with the praise. 'I guess we just do what we have to do.'

'Yes, but you don't need to get saddled with the blame for someone else's mistake.'

'Never mind. I'll set Dr Silvermark straight later. Right, let me get you sorted out so I can assist our new ENT with the rest of his clinic. He's good. I don't want this one to leave.'

'Do you have to help him every time he's here?'

'No. It's only for this week, thank goodness. The board

thought it good for the patients to have a sort of crossover. It's not my favourite thing to do and I doubt Dr Silvermark's happy about it, either. It's as though I'm looking over his shoulder, making sure he's good enough to work here.'

'You should have done that with Dr Bean. Perhaps he wouldn't have been here so long.'

'Yes. That's the other reason why the board suggested the transition period, but it's only for this week. Next week it's back to normal regarding my workload.' Claire stretched her arms over her head and sighed.

'He handled Pierce quite well, although it was easier once you arrived.'

Claire nodded and shook her arms before putting her hands in her pockets. She looked down at Pierce who was still playing in his own little world. 'That's because Pierce knows me.' She pondered the boy for a moment. 'I think what we need to try now is to break down all the instructions you give Pierce into little steps. Here, let me show you.' She crouched down and did what Dr Silvermark had done, picking up a car and driving it up to Pierce's truck. 'Hey, you look like a big truck. What have you got in the back? Dirt? Mud? Sand?'

'Lots of mud,' Pierce responded.

'Wow. You must be really strong.'

'I am. I'm the strongest truck in the whole wide world.'

'That's so cool. Brrrmmm...' She moved the truck around then spoke in her normal voice. 'It's time to go now, Pierce. It's time to pack up the toys and go home with Mummy.' Claire drove the car into the toy box, hoping Pierce would follow suit.

'It's time for play group,' Eileen said helpfully.

'Pierce?' Claire called his name and once more lifted his chin so his face was opposite hers. Still, he didn't look at her. 'Pierce? Can you look at me, please?'

Slowly he lifted his gaze from the truck and met Claire's impatiently.

'Good boy. Can you do some jobs for me, please?'

'OK.' He didn't sound impressed at being interrupted but at least he was listening.

'Can you pack up the toys, then go and get some special medicine, then go to play group?' Claire counted the jobs on her fingers.

'Yes.'

'All right.' She held up the first finger. 'Can you tell me what the first job you need to do is?'

Pierce thought. 'Pack up the toys.'

'Yes. And the next?'

'Um… Oh, I know. Get some medicine.'

'Very good. Do you remember what came after that?'

'Go to play group.' Pierce clapped his hands, knowing he was right.

'Correct.' Claire stood. 'If you can do the first job—put away the toys. I'll have one last reward for you.'

'A red one?' Pierce asked, quickly packing away the toys.

'Yes.' Claire looked at Eileen. 'Well, that worked.'

'Breaking everything into little steps?'

'Exactly. Try that for now—it should help. And make sure he makes eye contact with you. Try three steps at a time, you don't want to overload him. We'll have a better idea of exactly how to deal with the auditory processing difficulty once he's seen the audiologist.'

Pierce stood up, having finished putting away the toys.

Claire held out the prescription to him. 'Here's the instructions for the pharmacist. Can you hold them and look after them?'

'Yes.'

'Excellent.' Claire handed over another red jelly bean. 'You've been a good boy today, Pierce. Thank you.'

Pierce shoved the sweet into his mouth and held the script in his hand. 'What colour is the medicine?'

'I think it's pink.'

'No more drops?'

'No. No more drops. Just yummy pink medicine.'

'Do they have green?'

Claire stopped to consider for a moment. 'They might but the pink one is the super-duper medicine. It's as strong as the truck you were playing with.'

'Ooh.' The little boy thought for a moment. 'The green medicine must only be as strong as the car.'

Claire nodded. 'How very smart of you.'

'I need truck strong medicine 'cause I'm big and strong.'

'Yes, you are. All right. Now, can you tell me what your two jobs are?'

'Get the medicine. Go to play group. I know, I know.' He rolled his eyes at Claire as though she was silly.

'Nothing wrong with his intellect,' Claire said with a smile.

'Say goodbye to Dr Claire.'

'Bye Dr Claire,' Pierce said, his tongue and lips now quite red from the sweets. Claire waved goodbye, wrote in Pierce's notes, signed and printed her name and then took them out to Bethany.

'So how was that?' Bethany asked softly. The waiting room was now full of patients so Claire just smiled and nodded. 'Ah, that means we'll discuss it later. OK. Dr Silvermark's in clinic room one. He's not with a patient, just wanted to have a quick read of the notes and a brief word with you.'

'Oh. All right.' Claire dragged in a breath, straightened her shoulders and went to clinic room one. This time she paused and knocked on the door.

'Come in.'

She went in and closed the door behind her.

He was sitting in a chair, casenotes open in front of him. He turned to look at her. 'Dr Neilson…or can I call you Claire?'

'Claire's fine.'

'I've just been reading through my next patient's notes and have realised I've made an error concerning young Pierce.'

'Oh?' So perhaps the man wasn't perfect after all.

'Yes. I wrongly assumed that you had prescribed the ear drops for him.'

'So I gathered.'

'I've been reading through these notes and realised the signature I saw on Pierce's notes doesn't match the one I've found here—which clearly has your name printed beneath. I'd like to apologise for the mistake.'

Claire frowned, watching him for a moment. 'Uh…apology accepted.'

'Then why are you still frowning?' He leaned back in his chair, a small smile on his lips, one eyebrow raised. Did the man realise just how handsome he was? He may have a baby face but it was a cute one.

'Because I'm surprised you said anything. You could have just left it.'

He shrugged. 'I made a mistake. I own up when I make mistakes.'

'An honest doctor.'

Declan's smile increased. 'My father always says it's easier to eat crow when it's warm.'

Claire found herself responding to that smile. Not so pompous either. 'You know, I think I'm going to have to re-evaluate my opinion of you, Dr Silvermark.'

He stood, his enigmatic smile still in place, causing her knees to quiver a little. 'I hope that's a good thing.'

'So do I.' They stood there, grinning at each other.

'Shake my hand again.' Declan held out his hand. Claire hesitated. The last time she'd touched him she'd felt a powerful awareness, not only of him but of her own reaction to him. She wasn't sure touching him again so soon was wise.

'Why?'

'Because I thought it would be good to start again. Re-introduce ourselves.'

Claire swallowed, knowing it was easier just to go through the motions and keep herself under control than to refuse and have him ask why. Once more, when her hand slid into his the sparks were there. His warm fingers encircled hers, holding her hand firmly. He exerted a slight pressure as his gaze met hers.

'Declan Silvermark.' His tone was gentle.

'Claire Neilson.' She felt like cringing as her words came out almost as a breathless whisper. She needed to remove her hand, to break the contact. Her body was zinging to life as her overall awareness, not just of his touch but of him as a man, increased. His spicy male scent wound itself around her in an intoxicating manner. Her gaze flicked from his eyes to his mouth and back again, but not before noting his lips were now curved into a sexy and seductive smile.

When she tried to pull back, he added a little more pressure to her hand. Who was this woman? 'You feel that. Don't you, Claire?' His words were soft, barely audible, but she'd heard them, loud and clear.

'Huh?' Her eyes widened, unable to believe for a moment what he was actually saying.

'Nothing.' He didn't move. Didn't try to break the contact, which surprised her.

'No.' Claire slowly shook her head. 'There's no "nothing". What do you mean?' It wasn't like her to push and certainly not on this sort of topic with a colleague she'd just met, but for some reason she found it hard not to.

Declan held her gaze and swallowed. 'There's…chemistry between us.'

Claire was surprised, to say the least, that he'd said those words out loud. Getting a man to admit anything he was feeling was like getting blood from a stone, yet here was Declan Silvermark, less than an hour after she'd met him, saying such amazing things. 'You *are* honest. Aren't you,' she stated, a little confused.

He shrugged and frowned. 'I've been told it can be a little disconcerting at times.'

'Well, this is definitely one of them.' Taking a breath and knowing they needed to break the moment, she glanced down at their hands. 'You need to let go.'

'I know.' But he didn't and he wasn't sure why. Perhaps it had something to do with the way her soft and supple skin felt against his. Yes, he was honest but he wasn't used to being *this* honest with a woman he'd just met. His throat went dry and he swallowed once more.

Claire watched the action of his Adam's apple with interest, unsure what had come over both of them. 'We have a very busy clinic to get through.' This was so unlike her.

'And we're already running late.' He exhaled and took a step away, their hands still gripped as though letting go would mean letting go of this strange bubble they found themselves in where both seemed to be acting out of character.

'I'd like to apologise for being delayed this morning.'

Declan shrugged and edged further away, their arms now stretched, their fingers slowly slipping apart. 'It happens.' He paused and gave her hand one last squeeze. 'It's been nice to meet you, Claire.' With one final step, the contact broke. Declan cleared his throat, his gaze still holding hers. 'Shall we begin?'

As he said the words, she wasn't sure whether he was referring to the clinic or to exploring the attraction between them.

'Yes,' she replied, wondering if he knew she was tempted to agree to both.

CHAPTER TWO

THANKFULLY, the clinic continued without further incident and by one o'clock they were done.

'Not too bad,' Declan said as he wrote up the last set of case-notes. 'You've got a lot of cute kids in Mt Black.'

'Thanks, but I can't take credit for all of them.' They were both sitting at the nurse's desk, Declan finishing off the paperwork from his clinic while Claire was sorting through files for her own afternoon clinic, which would start very soon.

Declan raised his eyebrows, his gaze automatically going to her left hand. Was she married? He hadn't bothered to notice before, he'd been too busy trying to understand what was going on. He'd told a strange woman—a colleague, no less—that there was chemistry between them. Surely, if she was married, she'd have said something then. Wouldn't she? He needed to get control over his hormones and bring whatever relationship he was going to have with Claire back onto a professional footing because, in all honesty, that was all he had time for. Professional, courteous and light-hearted friendships with colleagues. That was the way he liked to keep it as it brought less stress. Then again, he'd already stuffed that up with his earlier comments. Control. He needed to regain control. Declan shifted in his chair, sitting up straighter.

'Should you?'

She shrugged. 'I delivered some of them. Pierce, for example.'

He was surprised. 'You don't have a midwife here?'

'Sure we do, and a paediatrician who does a weekly stint just like you, but babies have a habit of being born at times when people are either busy or not around.'

'And as GP, that means you've delivered a few.' Declan nodded.

'Exactly.'

'How many GPs does the hospital employ?'

'Full time?' she queried.

'Yes.'

'One.'

'One!'

'Uh-huh.'

'And I guess that's you.'

'You guess right.'

'But there are others. Right? You're not the only GP in Mt Black?'

Claire grinned. 'No. There are GPs who consult privately but—'

'You're the only one here full time,' he finished, his opinion of her increasing. That was quite a workload for one doctor, although he could already tell that she lived for her job. She was a natural, caring person. He'd noticed that and more during the time he'd spent with her and the patients that morning. She gave, not just medical help or assistance to everyone who needed it but rather a *personal* level of care. In his professional life and even in his private life, meeting people who were genuine had become a rarity.

'Every day. Like clockwork.'

'Although this morning the clock wasn't running on time?' He smiled, unable to resist the temptation to tease a little.

Claire glanced over at him and returned his smile, although he noted it didn't reach her eyes. She looked tired. 'I've already apologised for running late.'

'Yes, you did.'

'You don't know me, so don't tease. Not at least until the end of the day.' This time the smile did sparkle in her eyes but it quickly dimmed.

'Fair enough.' Declan closed the notes he'd finished and gave her his full attention. 'Problem at home?' He tried to make the question sound as natural as possible. In reality, he was becoming more and more curious about her with every passing second, which was unlike him. He wasn't in the habit of making friends easily but here he was, wanting to get to know his new colleague— a woman he'd known for half a day. Was she married? She didn't wear a ring but perhaps she'd taken it off for clinic. He'd known colleagues who'd done that. Did she have children? She'd certainly been very good with their young charges that morning.

'Nothing I can't handle…I think.'

'You think? Doesn't sound too positive.'

'Does everything need to be positive?'

'It certainly helps. Smile.'

'What?'

'Smile.'

'Why?'

'Because if you smile, even when you're not happy, your mind *thinks* you are and releases endorphins. Once the endorphins are released, you relax more easily.'

'And I suppose once I've relaxed, I'll think more positively?'

'It's worth a go. Besides, although we've just met, I'll let you in on a little secret.'

'What's that?'

Declan leaned forward to whisper but the moment he did he realised his mistake because Claire's scent wound itself about him and for one split second he forgot what he'd been about to say. Thankfully, the fog lifted a little and he remembered.

'I'm a good listener.'

Claire eased back slightly, trying to fight the attraction to that spicy scent he wore. She looked into his eyes and then wished she hadn't because she knew she could quite easily sit there all day, just staring into those hypnotic blue eyes. 'Is that so?' She cleared her throat.

'Yes.'

She usually didn't trust strangers but there was something about Declan Silvermark that she was drawn to. Was it because he'd been showing his honesty? She wasn't sure, but either way she was about to take a chance by confiding in him.

'OK, then. I have teenager trouble.'

Declan baulked at that. '*You* have a *teenager*? How old are you?'

Claire laughed at his unabashed reaction. 'Well, that's an interesting way of finding out my age.'

Declan cleared his throat, flummoxed by his own behaviour. 'Claire. I'm so sorry.' He shifted in his chair. 'That was rude of me.'

'No. It's all right. You're new here so you don't know the Neilson tragedy story.'

'There was a tragedy?' His tone was gentle and he immediately felt for her.

Claire recognised the empathy in his eyes and once more didn't feel embarrassed or worried about opening herself up. 'I don't *have* a teenager…well, I do but I didn't give birth to him. My parents died just after I turned eighteen, leaving me guardian of my five siblings.'

'Wow. You're one of six?'

'Very good, Declan. Five plus one is six. Good to know you can count,' she joked, used to people's reaction. 'In this day and age, if people have more than two children, it's considered brave or even abnormal.'

'Agreed.'

'How many siblings do you have?'

'Two, but they're a lot younger than me. I was an only child until I was sixteen.'

'Sounds intriguing. Are they your half-siblings?'

'No. No. We all have the same parents but I didn't meet my father until I was fourteen. Then my parents got remarried and the rest, as they say, is history.'

She heard the warmth and happiness in his tone when he'd spoken about his family. It was nice to hear. A lot of men she met, especially those in their late twenties or early thirties, rarely spoke of their parents. They treated them with a sort of indifference that made her feel sick. She would give anything just to have one more day with either of her parents. Anything. She swallowed over the lump that had suddenly appeared in her throat. 'You're close?'

'Very.' Declan paused. 'I imagine you're close to your siblings.'

'Yes. All we have is each other.'

'I take it the teenager is one of the youngest?'

'Brett *is* the youngest.' Her sadness disappeared and she smiled as Brett's features came to mind. Out of all of her brothers, he was the one who looked the most like her father and lately, when she looked at him, she began to really miss having her dad around. 'Sometimes I feel sorry for him. The poor kid has had three mothers and two dads. We all boss him around. We all tell him what to do.'

'And all he'd see is the injustice, not the love.'

Claire nodded, amazed he understood. 'Yes. Exactly.'

'My sister and brother—they're twins—turn to me for guidance sometimes. Most of the time I have no idea what to say so I tell them they're both smart and if they stop and think things through, they'll come up with a good answer.'

'You sound more gentle than I am.'

'Sure, because I'm still the big brother. You were forced into the mother role. How old is Brett?'

'Seventeen.'

'Oh, what fun.'

'Tell me about it.'

His voice gentled. 'He would have been so young when your parents died. That means you're the only real mother figure he can remember.'

'I guess.'

Declan's admiration for the woman beside him continued to increase. She worked at the hospital, probably a lot longer than any of the powers that be realized, or recognised for that matter, and then she went home to a house full of family. 'I'm sure you've done a wonderful job. Does everyone still live together or have they all branched off?'

'Five of us are at home. Mary, she's the second oldest, got married two years ago. Brett's the last one at school and he's talking about going to uni on the Gold Coast.'

'To study or party?'

Claire laughed but it ended in a sigh. 'A bit of both, I guess, although he's still not sure what he wants to study. I'd be surprised if he left. He's a real homebody but at the same time he's got this bee in his bonnet about leaving and doing stuff on his own.'

'Sounds…bold.'

'I'm not sure how we're all going to handle it if he does go but we'll have a family conference and cross that bridge when we come to it. Until then, I need to get him through his final year of school.'

'The study schedule is gruelling.'

'To say the least.'

Declan paused. He wanted to see more of Claire and preferably away from the hospital. This was uncharted territory for him and for someone who didn't take easily to change, he decided he wanted to ask her out. He swallowed over his suddenly dry throat and wiped his hands on his trousers, telling himself to relax before saying, 'Claire…this might sound strange but would you like to have dinner with me tonight?

'Di-dinner?' Claire stammered, totally shocked.

He smiled, drawing confidence from her reaction. 'You know. The meal between lunch and breakfast. Usually eaten in the evening, sometimes at a restaurant.'

She wasn't sure what to say. It was difficult to remember the last time a handsome man had asked her to dinner. Was he just being polite? Perhaps he wanted to discuss the hospital and protocols?

When she didn't answer right away, Declan continued, 'It's OK. You probably already had plans for tonight. Forget I asked.'

'No,' she blurted. 'I was just thinking things through.'

Good. He liked a woman who did that. Another point in her favour—even if she said no.

'I'm sorry but I can't have dinner with you tonight.'

'Already got a hot date?'

She smiled. 'Only with Brett's study books. He has mock exams starting tomorrow and he's stressing about them.'

'I can help. What I mean is, I'd be more than happy to help out. What's the subject?'

'English. One of the ones I'm *not* good at.'

He shrugged. 'I am.'

'An ENT who knows his way around Shakespeare? You're *that* smart, eh?'

'Actually, yes. I did med school in three years but that's not the point. The point is that you have responsibilities and I appreciate that. I'm more than happy to offer my services, in return for a meal.'

'So you just invite yourself to dinner.'

'I'll buy dinner. For the whole family. Give whoever's turn it is to cook a night off.'

'Do you always move so quickly?'

Declan thought about this for a moment. 'Er, no. This is quite out of the ordinary for me, although I always think through the variables. It's rare that I make an uncalculated decision.'

'Heaven forbid you should do that,' she teased lightly. 'So why do you want to help?' Claire couldn't help the scepticism. She was highly protective of her family and she doubted that would ever change. For as long as she could remember, they'd always come first.

'Because your brother Brett needs help. Study, I understand. Homework, I understand. Stress, pressure and anxiety, I definitely understand. If I can help him, please, let me.' This was new for him, he realised. It was refreshing to meet someone who didn't know his IQ level first. He was used to always being asked to help, to figure things out, but this time he had to beg to help. It was a novel experience and in some ways it actually felt good, rather than it being expected of him.

'Who needs help?' Bethany asked as she walked in, carrying her coffee-cup.

'It's nothing,' Claire said. 'Patients here?'

'Lining up and ready to roll.'

'You've got another clinic now?' Declan turned to face Claire.

'Yes. So it will be very late when I get home.'

He pondered this. 'Well, why don't I help?'

'With what?'

'With the clinic.' He looked at Bethany. 'That wouldn't be against hospital rules, would it? After all, I am registered to work here, which means I can prescribe medication.' He turned back to Claire. 'You've spent the entire morning seeing how I deal with patients so you shouldn't have any worries about me doing the wrong thing, and we'd get through your list in half the time. Unless I'm supposed to be somewhere else?'

Bethany shook her head. 'You're free.'

Claire found herself staring at him again. 'Why? Why would you do that?'

In that moment Declan received a startling insight into just who Dr Claire Neilson really was. She was a woman who'd been dealt a terrible set of cards but had made the most of them. She wasn't used to people simply doing something nice for her and the thought bothered him more than he cared to admit. It made him want to do *more* for her, to make sure that other people treated her right as well.

'Why help you?' Declan clarified, then smiled. 'Because I'm a nice guy.'

Claire laughed, shaking her head. 'All right. I guess it might help you to get to know some more of the locals, even though it isn't an ENT clinic. You'll probably see a few of them tomorrow in your adult clinic.'

'Well, if we find any today who need my expert attention, we'll deal with them straight away.'

'OK.'

Bethany stood there, looking from one to the other as though she were watching a tennis match. 'So, are we ready to start this clinic? Because the waiting room is bursting at the seams.'

'Lead the way,' Declan said, and waited for both women to precede him from the room. He rubbed his hands together excitedly. 'It's been a long time since I've done a general clinic.'

Claire laughed again. The man really was quite, quite strange. 'It's not that exciting, Declan.'

'Maybe not for you, but I'm looking forward to examining someone's big toe or even palpating an abdomen. Something different from ears, noses and throats.'

'You're not bored with your work, are you?'

'No, no. I like my specialty, which is why I chose it, but all I'm saying is a change is as good as a holiday.'

'You are one strange man, Declan.'

Declan merely smiled, noting that had been the first time she'd used his first name. He liked the way it sounded coming from her lips. He picked up a set of casenotes, calling his first patient through.

The clinic went well and Claire was astounded at how quickly they got through the list. At one stage she bumped into Bethany, who was coming out of a treatment room, pulling off a pair of gloves.

'How are we doing?' Claire asked.

'Last I checked, the waiting room was empty and I've just finished tidying up after changing Mrs Patterson's dressing.'

'Really? How was Mrs Patterson today?'

'A little shaky, but I'm not sure whether that was from seeing the dishy Dr Declan or from her Parkinson's—at least, that's what she said.' Bethany chuckled.

'Is she still here?'

'She's probably in the car park with her son, if you wanted to catch her.'

'No.' Claire shook her head. 'Although it's wonderful having Declan helping me in the clinic, it's strange not seeing everyone and catching up with them.'

'You can catch up with them next week when you start your afternoon clinic on time.' Bethany headed over to the receptionist desk and checked the list. 'Five more patients and we're done.' The door to the clinic opened as the nurse spoke and in walked Caroline Fitzsymonds.

'Hi, Caz,' Claire greeted her, picking up Caroline's file. 'Come right in.'

'Already?' Caroline whispered in surprise, and indicated the book in her hand. 'I was looking forward to reading at least a chapter before seeing you.'

Claire smiled. 'I have help today.'

'Really?' The two women walked to a clinic room. 'Who?'

'The new ENT.'

'Oh. Is he better than Dr Bean?' Caroline asked cautiously.

'Definitely. I hear your voice is still giving you trouble.'

'Yes. It comes and goes. My throat is fine, doesn't feel sore. I just can't talk.'

'Is Lenny enjoying the peace and quiet?' Claire sat down at the desk and motioned for Caroline to take the seat opposite her.

The two women had known each other since their schooldays and three years ago Claire had been a bridesmaid at Caroline and Lenny's wedding.

Caroline laughed. 'Just the other day he kept asking if he'd done something wrong. He said I was being so quiet he thought I was ignoring him because I was huffy about something.'

Claire chuckled. 'Sounds as though he has a guilty conscience.' She picked up her medical torch and a tongue depressor. 'Let's have a look.' Claire checked Caroline's throat and then examined the glands and sinuses on her face. 'You said your throat hasn't been sore?'

'No. I just can't talk.'

'How long for?'

Caroline thought. 'About four weeks.'

Claire nodded. 'OK. Your throat doesn't look bad. Usually, when there's an infection, it can get quite red and pussy but your glands aren't swollen and your sinuses feel fine.'

'So what do you think it is?'

'I think you've hurt your vocal cords in some way. Aren't you in the church choir?'

'Yes, but I hardly think that's taxing on the old vocal cords.'

'Well…as we have an expert in the hospital, why don't we ask him?'

'You mean I get to see the new ENT?'

'Sure.'

'I don't need to make an appointment in his clinic?'

'Actually, his clinic tomorrow is full. He said if there were any ENT cases today, he'd deal with them stat.'

'Stat?' Caroline chuckled. 'You sound like one of those doctors on TV when you say it like that.'

Claire smiled and stood. 'Wait here. I'll see if he's free.' She left her room and went to knock on the door to clinic room two. If only the hospital could get with the programme and put phones in each room, it would make life easier. Then again, there usually weren't two doctors on at once so there was no need, and if there wasn't a need, the hospital didn't bother.

'Come in,' he called, and Claire opened the door. It was the room she'd first seen him in that morning. Back then he'd seemed stiff and unnatural. Now he almost blended with the room as though he'd been consulting in it for years. It was a strange feeling.

He was with a patient. 'Sorry to bother you, Declan. Hi, Mr Francis. Sorry to intrude.'

'That's all right, lassy,' Mr Francis said, standing. 'We were done, weren't we, Doc?'

'Yes. Make sure you make another appointment to see Dr Neilson next week.'

Mr Francis smiled, his eyes twinkling as his gaze encompassed Claire. 'Wouldn't miss seeing her for the world. Was a little put out at having to miss seeing her today. She's one of the bright sparks in my week is little Claire, but here she is and it's good to see your smiling face, lassy.' Mr Francis took Claire's hand in his and patted it.

'How's Katie?'

'Ah, she's good. She's good. She's been a bit under the weather but the vet says she'll be as right as rain soon enough.'

'Good to hear. You take care, now, and I'll see you next week.' Claire smiled as the old man left.

'Katie's the dog, I hope?' Declan asked once their patient had gone.

'Be a bit of a problem if he was taking his wife to the vet.' Claire chuckled. 'Listen, I have a consult for you in room one. She's an old friend from school and her voice has almost disappeared. Throat, glands and sinuses appear unaffected.'

'OK.' They walked in together to find Caroline sitting in the chair, reading her book.

'Caz, this is Declan Silvermark.'

Caroline lazily looked up and then almost dropped her book. 'Wow, Claire. You're right. *Much* better than Dr Bean,' she said in a hoarse whisper.

Claire felt her cheeks go pink at her friend's words. 'I was speaking professionally,' Claire muttered between gritted teeth, not wanting Declan to think they'd been discussing him. Declan merely nodded politely and held out his hand. 'Hi. Glad to hear I'm better than Dr Bean, and I haven't even started my examination.'

Caroline shrugged. 'Sorry. I didn't mean to blurt that out.' When Declan didn't make any other comment, Claire began to relax, but as soon as Caroline spoke again, the tension increased once more.

'So I take it you'll be visiting Mt Black on a regular basis?'

'That's the plan.'

'One week every month?'

Claire frowned. Why was Caroline so interested?

'That's correct.'

'Well, then, one time when you're here, Lenny and I will simply have to have you and Claire around to dinner. Lenny's my husband,' Caroline added by way of explanation.

Declan's blue eyes twinkled as he met Claire's gaze but thankfully he didn't say anything. All she wanted was for the floor to open up and swallow her. 'Stop talking, Caz,' she told her friend. 'You're not doing your vocal cords any good.'

Caroline chuckled but did as she was told. Declan picked up a tongue depressor and medical torch, performing the same examination as Claire had. 'Right. As all the equipment I need is still set up from this morning's clinic, I think I'll take a closer look at your throat. What I'll be doing is putting some local anaesthetic in both your nostrils, which will slide down and numb the back of your throat. I can then insert a small camera down to see what's happening with your vocal cords.'

'What's your guess?' Caroline asked.

'Nodules.'

'That's what Claire said.'

Declan once more glanced at Claire. 'From what I've seen, she's an excellent doctor.'

'Oh, yes. Our Claire is the best. Everyone here loves her to bits.'

Declan smiled politely. 'So I'm coming to realise.'

'Feel free to join the club,' Caroline continued, and Claire shot her a warning look, feeling her cheeks getting hot.

'Is there a membership waiting list or do I need to go through a selection committee?' Declan deadpanned, and Claire found it difficult to meet his gaze, although she could hear the humour in his voice. She needed air and although she didn't think it was wise to leave two forthright people alone together, she walked to the door.

'I'll let Bethany know you'll be needing her assistance.'

'She's redoing Mr Francis's dressing,' Declan said. 'Can you assist, please?'

She'd almost been free. All she needed was a few minutes to get herself under control again. 'Uh…sure. I'll get the anaesthetic spray for you.'

'Thanks.'

Claire shot out of that room as though her white coat were on fire. Entering the small supply room, she walked through to where the medications were stocked and found the special can of local anaesthetic Declan had used that morning on a few of his young patients. Collecting a new sterilised nozzle for the end, she took them back to Declan.

He administered the anaesthetic while Claire helped Caroline to keep as still as possible, which wasn't easy when people were shoving tubes up your nose.

'Right. I'll go fire up the equipment and meet you in the second treatment room.' Declan walked out.

'You can go sit in the waiting room again if you like,' Claire said. 'Read your book, keep quiet and, for goodness' sake, stop trying to set me up with Declan.'

'Why not? He's gorgeous.' Caroline swallowed again. 'My throat feels strange,' she whispered.

'It should. Don't talk. Just relax and read.'

Caroline nodded and went out. Claire called her next patient through and managed to finish with them by the time Declan declared he was ready to do the procedure on Caroline. She accompanied her friend into the treatment room and held her head steady whilst Declan inserted the camera. Caroline coughed a few times, which was a natural reaction.

'Feels as though someone's shoving a bee up my nose,' she choked.

'Take it easy, Caz. Try and relax.' A moment later, Claire could see quite clearly on the monitor what the problem was. Definitely nodules.

Declan angled the monitor so Caroline could see. He pointed, showing her. 'See. This is what's been giving you the trouble. The nodules are basically calluses, just like you'd get on your hands if you'd been working in the garden for too long.'

Once he was satisfied nothing else was causing the damage, he removed the camera and let Caroline gently blow her nose. 'Let's return to Claire's clinic room to discuss things.' When they were there, he pulled up a chair next to Claire's. She could feel the heat emanating from his body, that spicy scent of his weaving its way about her senses again, and she knew that by the end of the week, every time she smelt that same smell, she'd think of Declan. And she didn't *want* to think of Declan.

'Definitely nodules, as I said, and I think we can treat these nodules non-invasively and in time they'll go away.'

'How do I do that?'

'Well, for starters, no yelling, no singing and no talking all day long.'

Claire chuckled at the impossible look on Caroline's face. 'You've just taken away her three favourite things.'

'You know, I hear that a lot when I prescribe this treatment. Also, pineapple juice is excellent for throats,' Declan continued.

'That's it? No talking and drink pineapple juice?'

'Basically. You need to keep your throat as moist as possible. When you have a dry throat and you talk, your vocal cords end up smashing against each other, especially when there's no lubricant. That is how the nodules form in the first place.'

'How am I supposed to keep my throat wet? Swallow a lot?'

'Increase your fluid intake. Try chewing gum.'

'A doctor is telling me to chew chewing gum.' Caroline looked at Claire and shrugged. 'Great. That'll fix my throat, but what about the ulcers I'll get?' She chuckled. 'What next?'

Declan smiled. 'Go home and try and relax. See Claire next week if things haven't settled. I'd like to review you when I'm here next so we'll book you into the ENT clinic.'

Caroline stood. 'That's it?'

'That's it. Try to whisper gently because even a harsh whisper is the same as yelling.'

'Oh, Lenny's just going to love this,' Caroline groaned, but nodded. 'I'd better go buy myself some pineapple juice and chewing gum. What about bubble gum? Is that all right?'

Claire smiled. 'I don't think it matters, so long as you're keeping your throat moist.'

'That's right,' Declan agreed as he wrote in Caroline's notes. 'I'll see you next time in my clinic.' He stood and headed for the door.

Caroline nodded and smiled as he left. 'He's a dish,' she told Claire.

'Yes, and he told you to stop talking.'

That didn't stop her friend. She grabbed a piece of paper, scribbled something down and handed it to Claire.

'"You like him, don't you?"' Claire read out loud, then screwed her face up. 'I've only known the man for a few hours. Give it a rest, Caz. I'm not interested in relationships.'

Caroline snatched the piece of paper back and wrote again. 'I'm not talking about a relationship. He's cute, you like him. Why don't you go for it?'

'Go for what? He's a colleague,' Claire responded, and removed the pen from her friend's hand. 'Now, go and do as the dishy doctor said and I'll call Lenny later to make sure you're behaving yourself.'

'Bossy,' Caroline whispered.

'You've got that straight. Comes from being the oldest and having early responsibility. Now, go and let me finish my clinic.'

Thankfully, Caroline seemed content to let the subject of Declan drop but Claire knew it wouldn't last long. She continued with her clinic and was surprised when they finished fifteen minutes early.

'A new record,' Bethany said, as she picked up her car keys and handbag. 'I'll head off and leave you to close up.'

'Sure.' Claire nodded. 'I'll finish up here and then do a quick round before leaving.'

'See you both tomorrow.' Bethany headed for the door, winking at Claire and then quickly pulling a straight face when Declan looked at her.

'Goodnight,' he said. He waited until they were alone. 'Did she just wink?'

Claire rolled her eyes and groaned, not wanting to answer the question, but she had a feeling Declan wouldn't let her off easily. 'Yes, I believe she did. I'll make a note to give her an eye exam some time tomorrow. With our receptionist off with flu, it won't do if one of our best nurses comes down with a squint.'

Declan chuckled. 'You don't catch a squint like you catch a cold, Claire.'

'I thought you were an ENT, not an eye specialist.'

'And you are, eh?'

'I'm many things. You have to be out here.'

'I can imagine.' He stood and began to unbutton his white coat. Claire sat and watched the show, noting that his clothes beneath were still as pristine and perfect as they had been when she'd first seen him that morning. Was the man always so clean cut? She wondered how he'd look with his hair ruffled. She frowned, cancelling that thought immediately.

'OK.' He looked around. 'Where did Bethany put my jacket?'

'Over here.' Claire stood and headed towards a tall cupboard. She unlocked it and pulled out his jacket. 'Here you go.'

'Thanks.'

'So…you're leaving?'

He nodded. 'Heading back to the motel.'

She'd thought about the way he'd invited himself over for dinner during her clinic and had run through different scenarios as to why he shouldn't go home with her. Top of the list was the need to protect her family. They came first—in everything. Sure, Declan seemed trustworthy and honest but perhaps that was just a front. Perhaps he was really an axe-welding, homicidal maniac! She glanced surreptitiously at him and smiled at the notion. She needed to get home, to paint, to unwind her mind before it sent her round the twist with its loopy ideas. Having Declan back to meet her family and enjoy a meal wasn't an option, and he seemed quite happy to go along with that.

She frowned as she watched him gather his briefcase and check for his car keys. She was a little confused by him, actually.

He'd admitted there was chemistry between them, flirted a little with her, teased her, laughed at her and sort of invited himself back for dinner, and here he was, leaving at the end of the day as though whatever had transpired that day was over and done with. Wasn't he? Or perhaps it was because she'd never actually agreed to him coming around and disrupting her family.

'So, do you want to come back for dinner or not?' she found herself blurting out.

Declan stopped looking for his keys and watched her for a moment. 'Are you sure?'

'Yes.' She lifted her chin a little defiantly.

'Really? You don't sound it.'

Claire sighed and shrugged. 'Look, my brother Jason will be cooking dinner. There will definitely be enough for one more. Brett does need help with his schoolwork and, well, it wouldn't be good manners if I let the new ENT eat alone on his first night in town.'

'So you're doing this out of a sense of obligation.'

'And what if I am?'

There it was again. That slight raise of her chin, that defiance, her gaze almost daring him to contradict her. Declan liked it. He was also beginning to realise just what an extraordinary woman Claire was and that type of woman was definitely his type. His throat dried up at the realisation but he forced himself to nod politely. 'Then I accept.' He quickly located his keys.

Claire didn't move for a moment and neither did he. 'Well, then. I'd guess we'd better get going.' She collected her own bag and began switching off the lights as she pulled her keys from her bag.

He chuckled. 'That's what I like. A gracious hostess.'

'Hey, this is business. I feed you, you help Brett.' Claire slid a key into the lock before turning off the last light and waiting for Declan to leave the clinic rooms so she could lock the door behind them. They headed off down a corridor which connected the clinic with the rest of the hospital.

'Definitely a deal.'

She motioned to the keys he was carrying. 'I take it you have your car here?'

'Yes. I drove from Brisbane to Mt Black last night so I'd be nice and early for the clinic this morning.'

Claire stopped walking. 'You're not going to go on about why I was late, are you?'

'No. No. Completely done with that. I'm sure you had a very good reason.'

'I did.'

'You don't have to tell me about it,' he teased as they entered the hospital.

'Good. I wasn't going to.' She headed over to the nursing staff in charge of the wards and introduced Declan. Claire watched with wonder as the two women immediately smiled and began fussing with their hair and uniforms in self-conscious little ways. She looked at Declan, watching him smile politely at the other women but looking highly uncomfortable. She watched as his back became ramrod straight again. It was the man she'd met that morning. The pristine and slightly pompous Dr Silvermark.

Claire wandered up the corridor to quickly check on the three inpatients. Had she just witnessed Declan's defence? She shouldn't be surprised. Everyone had them but she'd thought he'd be more at ease, especially when women were preening in front of him.

Satisfied her patients were all settled and ready to be tucked in for the night, Claire headed back the way she'd come and collected Declan.

'Goodnight, Declan,' one of the nurses called, and waved sweetly to him.

Declan merely smiled politely and nodded before following Claire out into the warm spring night.

'Another woman to add to your fan club?' she quizzed.

Declan's eyebrows shot up. 'I have a fan club?'

Claire shook her head, a teasing smile on her lips. 'You must know that women fawn all over you wherever you go.'

'Now, if I knew that, Claire, you might call me conceited.'

'So, as you purposely choose to ignore it, I can call you naïve?'

He pondered that. 'Not naïve. Merely unwilling.'

'Ah, so you do know.' Claire grinned and stopped beside her

car, turning to face him. Their gazes meshed and held, the smile slowly slipping from her face. The atmosphere between them intensified, blocking out everything around them. She had usually felt awkward and a little flustered whenever moments like this had happened in the past but for some reason she didn't feel that way now. There was something about Declan, something that was different from other men.

She felt comfortable with him, being this close to him, having him inside her personal space, and was content to let the moment happen. It was a strange but wonderful sensation. Liberating, too.

'I may know but that doesn't mean I like it.'

'What man doesn't like being centre of attention?'

'I don't.'

'Come on. Of course you do.'

'No.' He shook his head emphatically. 'Honestly. I don't.' He rubbed his eyes, starting to feel the strain of the day. When he next looked at Claire it was to find her watching him closely.

Claire was once more struck by the vibrancy of his eyes. She could lose herself in those eyes and that was dangerous. Still, it didn't mean she couldn't appreciate them. Although the sun was almost down, the artificial light from the hospital, combined with the already shining moon, made him fit the description of tall, dark and handsome to perfection.

Slowly, he reached out a hand to caress her cheek with the backs of his fingers. He felt as though he'd known this woman for years instead of just a few short hours. He'd hardly exchanged any personal conversation with her and generally he was in the habit of really getting to know someone before he became involved. Sure, he'd been attracted to other women but with Claire…there was something different. Something he'd never come across before.

The touch was brief, over and done with so quickly she wondered if she'd imagined it.

'You're a strange man, Declan Silvermark.'

'And you're one beautiful woman, Claire Neilson.'

CHAPTER THREE

'THAT WAS an amazing meal.' Declan leaned back in his chair and looked at Claire's brother, Jason. 'You're a good cook.'

'I'm not a cook, I'm a chef…well, training.'

'I stand corrected.'

Jason stood and began gathering the plates, stacking them like a professional waiter. 'That's OK. It's a common mistake.' He carried them into the kitchen.

Declan leaned over to Claire. 'He's not offended, is he?'

'No. Jason is like you. Honest and more than willing to put people in their place.' She turned to face her youngest brother. 'Brett, ready to study?'

'Aw, come on, Claire. Now?'

'Well, when are you going to do it?'

'I told you this morning. I need help with it.'

Claire indicated Declan. 'And I've brought you some help. Apparently Declan is quite the whiz when it comes to English.'

Brett nodded grudgingly. 'Fine. I'll get my books.' But he didn't move.

Declan turned, giving Brett his full attention. 'What other subjects are you taking?'

'He's doing applied physics and chem,' Jason answered proudly as he came back for another round of plates. 'He's a smart one is our little bro.'

Declan watched the boy closely. Brett looked at his brother and for a moment there was veiled animosity in the teenager's eyes. Interesting. So Brett didn't like his brother speaking for him. Declan nodded. 'Let me guess. You can handle the toughest equation but writing a two-hundred-word paper gives you nightmares?'

'Yes!' Brett turned his astonished gaze on Declan.

'I know the feeling. Get your books and we'll have a look at it.'

'OK.' This time Brett did move. While Declan was waiting, he stood and picked up some dirty glasses.

'Leave that,' Claire said quickly. 'You don't need to do that.'

'It's fine, Claire.' His smile was polite before he turned away. Claire had been a little surprised during dinner just how little attention he'd paid to her. Not that she wanted to monopolise him, but he was *her* guest and yet he seemed more determined to ignore her and focus on getting to know her siblings. Perhaps they were a novelty to him? After all, he'd said he'd been an only child until the age of sixteen so there was a huge age difference between him and his brother and sister.

She touched her cheek, brushing her fingers over the area he'd caressed. It had been such a brief touch but it had felt incredible. She frowned and shook her head. This wasn't like her. She didn't act this way around men. She was usually the one in charge, the one calling the shots, the one saying what would happen next, but this time she was beginning to think she was out of her depth.

Claire realised someone was speaking to her. 'Yes? What?' She looked up at Mary, who had come over for dinner as her husband was working late that night. She was making the 'A-OK' sign with her thumb and forefinger together in a circle. Her sister winked.

'Way to go. He's gorgeous and nice and funny. We like this one.'

'He's a colleague,' Claire whispered quickly, her gaze on the doorway into the kitchen. She could see Elizabeth, Jason and Thomas becoming interested in Declan, but she knew she needed to keep it strictly business. 'That's all. Just a colleague who's new in town and so we have him over for a meal.'

'You didn't do that with Dr Bean when he first came.'

'That's because he was an idiot.'

'Who's an idiot?' Declan asked as he walked in.

'Dr Bean,' both sisters said.

'Oh. My predecessor. Well, I'd have to agree with you there. Just from reading his notes today, I could see that. In fact, there are a few cases I'll probably need to discuss with both you and the hospital's legal department,' Declan said meaningfully.

Claire grimaced but nodded. 'I'll arrange it.'

Brett came bounding down the stairs into the dining room, the table having now been cleared and wiped down. 'We can do it here,' he told Declan, thumping down his books and papers.

'Sure.'

Claire looked at Declan again. 'Thank you.'

'No prob. I help my brother and sister all the time.'

'You do?' Brett asked. 'What year are they doing?'

'Umm, sort of year nine, year ten.'

'Which one?' Claire asked.

'Both.'

'Both?' Claire and Brett spoke in unison.

'They're twins.'

'How old are they?' Brett asked.

'Fourteen.' Declan shrugged. 'They're gifted.'

It was then Claire remembered Declan saying he'd done medical school in three years. She'd thought he'd been joking but now she wasn't so sure. 'You were serious before?'

He raised an eyebrow and glanced up at her as he sat down at the table next to Brett. 'Which part?' There was delight in his gaze and Claire felt herself begin to blush. She wasn't talking about the moment they'd shared, or the way he'd tenderly caressed her face. He also knew exactly what she was talking about, she could sense it.

'Med school.'

He nodded once. 'Yes, I was serious.'

'What's your IQ?'

'Serious about what?' Brett wanted to know. Both Declan and Claire ignored him.

'It's high.' He didn't like talking about it. Over and over again he'd endured the prejudice that went hand in hand with being smart. Most days he could deal with it but at times like this, when he was relaxed and having a good time *and* being treated like a normal person, he definitely didn't want to talk about it.

'Declan, you did medical school in half the time it usually takes. That's unheard of.' Claire wasn't going to let him drop the subject that easily. If what he said was true, then he was a genius.

'Not anymore.'

'You did *what*?' Brett asked with total admiration. 'Way to go, dude.'

'Thanks.' Declan looked intently at Brett's books, firmly shifting the attention from himself. 'Now, where do we start?'

Mary called for Claire to help her in the kitchen and she walked off in a stunned silence, trying to figure the man out. If he was as smart as he'd said, then what was he doing practising as an ENT in Mt Black?

'He is *so-o-o* cute,' Mary whispered.

'Shh.' Claire glanced back the way she'd just come but knew Declan couldn't hear them.

'Who's cute?' Jason asked, coming in the back door.

'Shh.' Claire glared at him.

Jason paused and looked into the dining room before turning back to his big sister. 'Are you interested in him? You should go for it, Claire.'

'Go for what?' Elizabeth said, bounding into the room and throwing her arm around her twin's shoulder. She gazed at Jason. 'Are you making anything for dessert?'

'Wasn't going to.'

'You should,' Mary added. 'With a guest here, it will be nice to have something other than fruit or ice cream.'

'Well…' Jason thought for a moment. 'I have a new crème brûlée recipe I wanted to try out, but I'm not sure if I have enough cream.' He walked over and opened the refrigerator door.

Elizabeth licked her lips. 'Sounds good, bro.'

'Nope. Although…' he poked around in the fridge '…I could make a pavlova.'

'They take too long to cook,' Elizabeth complained. Mary and Claire rolled their eyes.

'We'll leave you to stack the dishes,' Mary said, linking her arm through Claire's. 'Will those two ever stop arguing?' she asked Claire.

'I thought it might wane when they grew up.' Claire sat down, exhausted from her day. 'Where's Thomas?'

'He volunteered to go and get Greg. Thanks for letting me stay for dinner.'

'Hey, even though you're married, Mary, this will always be your home.'

Mary smiled. 'I'm glad Greg was working late tonight, otherwise I might not have met Declan. He seems really nice.'

'Yes.' Claire frowned. 'Yes, he does.'

Mary laughed. 'You don't sound as though you believe yourself. Problem?'

'No. No.' Claire forced a smile. 'He's brilliant.'

'I can see that.'

'No. I mean *brilliant*. He did med school in three years.'

Mary nodded slowly, impressed. 'Wow.'

'Yeah. He's…'

'Intriguing?'

'Yes.'

'You like him. More than as a colleague. I can tell.'

'How?'

'Because I've never seen you quite so flustered or perplexed. Even with Ken.'

'Hmm.'

Mary sat up straighter in her chair. 'Why don't you go and get changed, and once he's finished helping Brett take him outside for a walk? Show him the barn.'

'The barn? How exciting.' Claire chuckled but it ended on a sigh. 'No. He'll probably want to head back to his motel soon.'

'I doubt it. He seems more inclined to stay the night if you give him half a chance.'

It was Claire's turn to sit up from where she was slouching on the lounge. 'Don't even say things like that, Mary. You'll give me palpitations.'

'Hmm. I wonder why. Now, go and get changed, take him for

a walk and get to know him a little better. Stop being the big sister and have some fun.'

'You're taking over the mantle?'

'Well, I *am* the second oldest. I'll finish getting everyone organised. Go.'

Claire knew she wasn't going to get a moment's peace from Mary until she did as she was told. Walking to her room on tired legs, Claire contemplated just falling onto the bed and sleeping but she knew she wouldn't. All her life she'd done what had been expected of her and now Mary was telling her to have some fun. She laughed humourlessly as she changed into jeans and jumper. Fun? What was that?

Declan couldn't help but admire Brett. The poor kid was in a difficult situation and if there was one thing all those psych classes he'd taken had taught him, it was to probe gently to get the best results.

'You've got a good brain,' Declan said, noting how easily Brett grasped the concept of structure.

'I just get muddled sometimes.'

'Do you think there's more to it than that?'

Brett slowly met Declan's gaze. 'Meaning?'

Declan said softly, 'How are your friendships at school?'

Brett shrugged. 'OK. I've known everyone, like, for ever.'

A slow smile came across Declan's lips. 'There's a girl in there somewhere.'

'No.' The denial was quick.

Declan merely raised his eyebrows, indicating he didn't buy it but he wasn't going to push any further.

'All right,' Brett said after a moment. He looked into the kitchen where his other siblings were and dropped his voice even lower. 'Her name's Courtney.'

'You've known her for long?'

Brett shook his head. 'Her family moved here about a year ago. All the guys like her.' After a pause, he continued. 'She sits next to me in English.'

'You've got to sit next to her tomorrow when you do your exam.'

'Yeah. What if I can't think straight? What if because she's just there I—?'

'You get all tied up in knots whenever you see her?'

'Yeah!'

'I know the feeling.' It was Declan's turn to glance towards the kitchen, where he saw Claire out the corner of his eye. She'd changed her clothes and had let her hair down from the ponytail she'd worn at the hospital. Long blonde strands cascaded down around her shoulders and Declan swallowed. 'I know the feeling.'

Brett followed his gaze. 'You like my sister?'

Declan turned his attention back to the teenager. 'I do, but we hardly know each other.'

'You should go for it.'

'What about you?'

Brett baulked. 'No way, man. I mean, I've got two more exams this week and this is *Courtney* we're talking about.'

'Pretty?'

'Amazing.'

'So why not ask her out? It's school holidays soon.'

'Nah. It'll never happen.'

'Why?'

'She's…normal, you know?'

'Meaning?'

'She has two parents.'

'Ah, and you don't.'

Brett shrugged. Declan paused and then jumped in. 'You're conscious that you're different.'

'Exactly. I mean, I was raised by my sisters and brothers. I love them and all but come on. Seriously? I could never bring Courtney here. She'd never understand. Plus, Claire would probably have a fit.'

'Maybe, maybe not.'

'Hey, if you start dating Claire, maybe that will soften her up.'

Declan laughed. 'I doubt it would work that way.' He glanced towards the kitchen again, loving the way Claire's face brightened when she laughed with her siblings.

'Does your stomach twist into knots when you look at her?' Brett asked.

'Yeah.'

'That's how I feel with Courtney.'

Declan nodded and turned back to Brett. 'Now, workwise… everything as clear as mud?'

Brett smiled. 'Yeah. You gotta go?'

'I think it might be time.'

'Thanks, Declan.'

'Not a problem. Let me know if you need any other help.' Declan stood.

'Did you really do med school in three years?'

'Yep.'

'Is it good, being smart?'

Declan smiled. 'Try asking yourself that question. You're no dummy, Brett. Quite the opposite, in fact. Now, get to work.' He held out his hand and Brett shook it.

'You won't tell anyone…'

'What we talked about? No.'

'Thanks.' Brett returned his attention to the books as Declan took in a calming breath and headed for the kitchen. The bright sibling laughter made him feel as though he'd outstayed his welcome. They'd fed him and he'd helped Brett. That was the deal and now the deal was done. He hated walking into a room where people were laughing and having a good time but he'd forced himself to do it in the past and he would do it now.

'Hi, there.'

Claire straightened from where she'd been leaning against the bench, chatting with Elizabeth, Jason and Mary. 'All done?'

'Sure. He's a bright kid.'

'Thanks.'

'You're welcome.' Declan walked over to the coat rack where he'd left his jacket and picked it up. 'Well, I'd better get going.'

Claire frowned, wondering why he was in such a rush. 'You're leaving?'

'I'm making dessert,' Jason added. 'You have to stay for dessert.'

'Thanks, but I think I've intruded long enough.'

'No way,' Mary said, coming to take his jacket from him. She hung it up again. 'You're staying for dessert and that's all there is to it, Declan.'

He glanced at Claire, wondering how she felt. She didn't seem to be protesting so he shrugged. 'I guess I am. Thank you.'

'Claire,' Mary continued, 'why don't you show Declan a bit more of our property?'

Claire gaped at her sister. 'It's dark out and I thought we were having dessert.'

'It'll be a while yet,' Jason said. 'I've just put it in the oven. Go for a walk.'

'Sure,' Elizabeth chimed in. 'Show him the barn.'

Claire shook her head, annoyed with her siblings for pushing.

'You don't have to,' Declan said, and she realised he'd mistaken her body language.

'It's OK. We can go. It's not far.'

Declan nodded and headed for the back door.

'Take your time,' Mary called out as they left. Claire let the back door slam shut on purpose.

'You all right?' Declan asked.

'Sure. Just annoyed.'

He nodded as they headed down the back path. 'Brothers and sisters have a way of doing that. If you don't want to go for a walk, we can just stay out here and chat for a while or go back in.'

Claire smiled, secretly pleased to have him all to herself for a while. 'It's fine. The barn's this way.' She indicated the paved path that led away from the house, down over a small rise.

'How big is this place? I was surprised at the distance it is from the hospital.'

'Meaning?'

'Meaning I was surprised at the distance from the hospital. No hidden meaning in that sentence, Claire.'

She sighed. 'Sorry. A few of the hospital board members think I should live closer.'

'What business is it of theirs?'

'My sentiments exactly.'

'As long as you're able to provide the care you're supposed

to, what does it matter? Doctors in Brisbane live a lot farther away than this.'

'I guess it's just small-town mentality.'

'They expect too much from you, Claire.'

She shrugged. 'I guess.'

'Yet you love your job.'

'I do. I really do, Declan.' She smiled, glad to be talking to him in this way, of just getting to know her colleague on a more personal level. Most of the other specialists who came to Mt Black to do their clinics were polite and good at their jobs, but that was as far as her connection with them went. Declan was proving to be very different and it was nice to have a medical colleague she could discuss things with, knowing he'd keep everything she said confidential.

'So, as I said, how big is this place?'

'Ten acres. My parents bought it just after they got married. They had a hundred acres and sold parcels of land off now and then. It provided them with enough money so that when they died, we weren't in debt.'

'A load off your mind, at least.'

'Yes.'

'It must have been tough, being in charge all of a sudden.' His voice was thoughtful, as though he could well imagine what it must have been like.

'I guess. I just did what needed to be done. One day after the next type of thing. Take each problem as it comes.'

'Your siblings are all wonderful. You've done a good job, Claire. You should be proud.'

She shrugged. 'I can't take all the credit. Mary's always been the peacekeeper and I'd have gone nuts at times if she hadn't stepped in.'

'She's second oldest, right?'

'Yes. She's three years younger than me and I guess she grew up overnight, too.'

'Jason and Thomas are the twins?'

'No. Jason and Elizabeth.'

'Oh. So where does Thomas fit in?'

'He's between the twins and Brett.'

'And who's Greg?'

Claire smiled. 'Mary's husband. They've been married for almost two years. They're living in town but they're building a house over there.' Claire pointed in an easterly direction. 'I can see one day we'll all have our own little houses, scattered around the ten acres.' She chuckled.

'Sounds nice. Close but not too close.' They came to a fence that had a little wrought-iron gate, which opened with a creak. 'So who gets the main house?'

'I guess I do. It's never really been discussed in great detail but on the few occasions we've talked about it, it's been assumed I'd end up with it. Don't know why. I think the person who ends up with the most kids should have it, and as twins runs in the family, who knows?'

Declan chuckled. 'Sounds feasible.' He looked out over the property, glad of the almost full moon giving them a decent amount of light. 'Not a working farm?'

'No. Hasn't been for many, many years.'

'The space, the scenery. It's all lovely.' He glanced down at her as he spoke and she wondered for a split second whether he was referring to her or the view before them.

Claire cleared her throat. 'The barn's this way.'

'What's so special about the barn?'

'You'll see.'

'Ah. Trying to keep me in suspense.'

Claire laughed. 'Is it working?'

'Yes, actually.' They were silent for a moment before he said, 'How many children would *you* like to have?'

Claire stumbled and then looked at him. Why had he asked that? Did that mean he was interested in her if he was talking about children? Her confused mind shifted into the correct gear and she realised he was asking the question in relation to her previous comment about the house.

'Uh…I wasn't planning on having any.'

'Is that to avoid getting lumbered with the big house?'

Claire looked at him. That wasn't at all the answer she'd expected. 'Er...no.'

'Oh. Then why? Or is it too personal?'

Claire shrugged and decided she may as well just blurt out the truth. The sooner he knew she wasn't in the market for a long-term relationship, the better. *If* he actually liked her that way, of course. The signals he was giving off were still very mixed. 'No. Well, not really. Brett was six when Mum and Dad died, and even before that I was always helping, from the time he was born.'

'You feel as though you've already raised your children?'

'Yes.' She was surprised he understood, then she remembered his intellect. 'Even though they're not technically mine.'

'That's understandable. My dad didn't ever want to have children and now look at him.' Declan chuckled. 'He's got three, and my brother Evan is *exactly* like the old man. I look like Dad but, personality-wise, I'm more like Mum. Helen, my sister, is the same temperament as us and is the dead spit of my mum.'

'It doesn't bother you that your dad didn't want kids?'

'No. He and my mum met and married when they were teen-agers. Dad was nineteen, Mum was eighteen. They married quickly and divorced just as quick. He had his reasons for not wanting children and when my mum discovered she was pregnant, she tried to find him, just to let him know, but it was as though he'd dropped off the face of the earth. As I mentioned, I didn't meet him until I was almost fifteen and...' he shrugged, recalling the moment he first met his dad '...we hit it off right away. It was as though I'd found a missing piece of me—a piece I didn't even realise was missing until I found it. Guess that doesn't make much sense.'

Claire shrugged. Having never really felt that way, she didn't understand what he was saying.

'Anyway, Dad changed his mind about having kids once he got used to having me around and now I'd have to say he's the best father in the world, but I guess I'm biased.'

Claire sighed nostalgically. 'What do your parents do?'

'They're both doctors.'

'Oh. Specialists?'

'No. GPs.'

'So where does the high IQ come from?'

Declan smiled and shook his head. 'I was wondering when we'd come back to that.'

'You don't like talking about it,' she stated.

'Not particularly. I have a high IQ. That doesn't define me and so many people think it does. I'm me. Declan. Not some kind of freaky person who just happens to understand concepts with ease.'

'You're sick and tired of everyone else viewing you as some sort of oddity?'

'Yes.'

'I know the feeling…although not in the same way.'

He nodded. 'Of course you do. Being responsible for five siblings at the age of eighteen—'

'Made me more than normal.' They reached the barn but Claire made no move to head inside. 'Sometimes I wanted to scream. I just wanted to be left alone to do what I needed to do.'

Declan nodded eagerly. 'Exactly. I know how that feels.'

'I guess you do.' They stood there, looking at each other in the moonlight.

'See. We do have things in common.'

'Hmm.' Claire shifted uncomfortably and gestured to the barn door. 'Wanna come in?'

'That's what I'm here for.'

She smiled as she opened the door and flicked on the light.

'Electricity.'

'Yes. A luxury Christmas present from my family a few years ago. Greg, Mary's husband, is an electrician. Come on in.'

Declan walked in, totally surprised. This was no barn. Sure, it looked like a barn from outside but inside it had been renovated and was now an artist's studio. The floor had a linoleum covering and comfortable old chairs were against one wall. Canvases and paints littered a workbench and an easel was set up in front of a window—a window that had light, gauzy curtains covering it. Along the back wall was a small sink, with a mixture of clean brushes in old coffee-jars. A kettle sat next to them and below the benchtop was a small bar fridge. He walked slowly into the room, looking around at everything, and made his way towards the painting on the easel.

'Yours?' he asked, pointing to the painting.

'Yes.'

'Your sanctuary.'

Claire smiled lovingly as she gazed around the room. 'Exactly. It's where I've had some personal revelations, some professional revelations and some of the most important conversations of my life.'

'With your siblings?'

'Yes, and other people.' She thought about Ken. He'd never quite understood this room or her need to paint. 'Usually, when I get time to come here, after a few hours of solitude one of them will come down and talk about something that's bothering them, or ask for advice.'

'They know you're relaxed.'

Claire laughed. 'They're usually hoping I'll say yes to whatever it is they want. The other day Brett asked when I was going to be painting next.'

'Uh-oh.'

'That's what I was thinking. He wouldn't talk to me up at the house. It's as though there's an unwritten rule down here. No judgements, no punishments. Just time to listen.' As she said the words, she wondered about the sleepless nights her brother had been having and the stress he felt about his exams. If she'd been more on the ball, she would have picked up on it and come down to paint just so he *could* talk to her.

'That's good.' Declan watched her facial expressions closely.

'Yes.' Claire trailed her hand over the bench. 'My dad built this bench, those shelves, put the plumbing in, converted this barn for me. It was a present for my eighteenth birthday.' She smiled at him. 'I love this place. It reminds me of them, but not in a sad way. More in a way that reminds me how rich I am…in blessings.'

Declan nodded and she saw complete understanding in his gaze.

'Personally, I think he was hoping to stop me from moving out of home.'

'Why?' Declan continued to look around the room.

She shrugged. 'I was…getting serious about a guy and that guy was going to Sydney to do his medical training.'

'Let me guess. The guy hightailed it when the accident happened.'

'Couldn't get out of my life fast enough.'

Declan walked to the shelves where a long row of canvases were kept. 'May I?'

'Sure.' Claire stood beside him as he flicked through them. Some were still life, some of the scenery around the house and around Mt Black. Some were portraits.

'Who's this?' He came to a canvas with a portrait of a man.

'Ken. Ex-fiancé.'

'Ah.' Declan studied the canvas. 'Nice strokes. You've captured the skin contours exceptionally well.'

'Thanks. I thought so, too.'

'What happened? To make him ex, I mean.'

Claire thought for a moment, wondering just how much to tell this man she'd only just met. 'The weight of my world. I don't think he ever really understood me.'

Declan nodded and moved on to the next canvas. It was a modern art painting, done with dark colours in a slashing jagged pattern. 'After the break-up?'

Claire chuckled. 'Yes. You're very good at interpreting art.'

'Your style makes it easy.' He flicked to the next one. 'How long ago did you break up with Ken?'

'Five years.'

Declan nodded and continued to look. 'Does he live in Mt Black or did he hightail it to Sydney as well?'

'No.' Claire smiled. 'Ken is happily married and works as the hospital's legal officer.'

'Ah. The man I need to chat with.' Declan nodded and looked at another painting. 'This is Brett?'

'Thomas, when he was eleven.'

'They look similar.'

'Yes. That was the day I told him about the birds and bees. Then, of course, Jason and Elizabeth—who were fifteen—added their own versions.'

Declan chuckled. 'I can imagine.' He looked at the next portrait and studied it a while. It was one of her parents. 'You're the spitting image of your mother.'

'I know. I'll often get patients who knew them telling me that.'

'She was very beautiful.' Declan looked at her, his gaze soft. 'You're very beautiful, too, Claire.'

She felt as though he'd tackled her to the ground as all the breath seemed to whoosh out of her. Her mouth went dry and she unconsciously wet her lips, swallowing. 'You've said that before.'

'And I'll probably say it again.' He paused, lowering his voice to a more intimate level. What Brett had said earlier about stomachs twisting into knots was very true. Declan was incredibly attracted to Claire and he couldn't stop his feelings. Learning to control his emotions to stop unwanted stress and anxiety was something he'd dealt with while growing up, but he'd also learned when to give way to his feelings and let them flow. 'Claire.' He left the paintings and walked closer. 'I want to kiss you.'

'Do you think that's a good idea?'

'Probably not.' He edged nearer with agonising slowness. Claire wasn't sure what to do. Should she push him away? Should she haul him against her? All she knew for certain was that he was evoking emotions in her she'd never felt before. He seemed to understand her, better than anyone else she'd ever met. It was uncanny, surreal but also such a relief. 'Do you want me to kiss you?' he murmured, his body almost pressing against hers, the heat radiating out.

'Hmm?' Claire replied weakly, her gaze flicking from his mouth back to his eyes.

'I said, do you—'

'I know, I know,' she whispered. 'I heard.'

'Going to answer the question?'

'Um…yeah.' He was so close, so wildly masculine, and she definitely craved a taste.

Declan smiled. 'Is that the answer or just a mumble?' He breathed in deeply, her intoxicating scent winding its way about him once more.

Claire couldn't wait any longer, her fingers reaching out to touch his warm chest tentatively. Closing her eyes, she marvelled at the sensation and felt a shudder course over her spine. Grabbing his tie, she tugged, urging his head down.

Finally. Declan pressed his lips to hers and she sighed into the kiss. This was good. This was nice. This was right even though she knew in her mind that it was very, very wrong.

The words kept going in a loop through her brain as his soft lips continued to gently tease and coax a response from hers. He didn't have to work too hard because she was more than willing to give as good as she was getting.

'Claire!'

The frantic cry came from outside, as though someone was running down towards the barn. Declan broke off and looked at her. 'Did you hear—?'

'Claire!'

'That's Brett.' Both of them rushed to the door just as Brett barrelled inside the barn.

'Claire!' He puffed. 'Quickly. Lizzie's burnt her arm. It's bad.'

CHAPTER FOUR

THEY all ran back up to the house, Claire's mind working overtime as Brett breathlessly told them what he knew.

'She was helping Jason and he told her to take the dessert out of the oven and then she was yelling and screaming and Mary told me to get you and to say that Lizzie had burnt her arm. I ran as fast as I could.'

Claire nodded and as they neared the house, she said, 'It's fine, Brett.' She could hear the panic in his voice. 'Lizzie will be fine. I'll make sure of that.' She flung open the back door to find Mary standing with Elizabeth at the kitchen sink, holding her arm beneath the streaming cold water.

'Let me take a look,' Claire said in her best calm doctoring voice. The instant she looked at her sister's arm, she felt her stomach twist and swallowed over the bile that rose in her throat.

'Claire?' It was Declan. The word was spoken softly and quietly but with the directness she needed. She glanced up and met his gaze. There was a question there. Was she able to handle this or did she need him to take over? He was letting her call the shots. After all, Elizabeth was her sister.

She cleared her throat and straightened her shoulders, shaking her head. Declan got the message and took over, allowing Claire to play big sister, which was exactly what Elizabeth needed. Declan walked over and took a look at Elizabeth's arm.

'Jason, call the hospital.' He spoke calmly but clearly. 'Let them know we're coming in. Mary, get plastic sandwich wrap and ice packs. We'll take my car.'

'What can I do?' The question came from Brett and Declan could almost feel the teenager's anxiety. It was certainly something Declan knew about as he'd had to deal with anxiety his entire life. He wondered if Claire knew about Brett. Right now, though, Brett needed to feel needed, to have a job to do to help him cope with what was happening.

'Come and comfort Elizabeth. Just put your hand here, on the back of her shoulder. Let her know we're going to take care of her.'

Claire took the sandwich wrap from Mary and rolled out a large piece, getting it ready. The burn, which could be seen below Elizabeth's sleeve, was turning a nasty shade of red. They needed to wrap the plastic around Elizabeth's arm so the air didn't get to it.

'Can I have some scissors, please?' Declan said quietly. A second later, Claire held out a pair to him just as she would have had she been handing them to him across an operating table. He glanced up and smiled. 'Thanks.'

'Wait,' Elizabeth said. 'What are you doing with them?'

'We need to cut your sleeve out of the way,' Claire explained.

'What? This top cost a fortune.'

'It's already ruined, Lizzie,' Claire pointed out, frustrated with her sister.

'I'll buy you a new one,' Declan promised. 'We need to get what fabric we can out of the way. Some of it is already stuck to your arm. I'll deal with that at the hospital.' Elizabeth's tears increased as Declan carefully cut the loose fabric from the area. 'Almost over. We'll have you bundled up and heading to the hospital in no time,' he soothed. She was a little more distraught than he'd anticipated and he wasn't sure whether it was because of the destruction of her top or the shock and pain of what had happened. He was watching for signs of hypovolaemic shock but didn't feel the burns were excessive enough to cause it.

'Hospital knows we're coming,' Jason said as he returned to his twin's side. 'It's OK, Lizzie. Hang in there, sis.'

Declan looked at Jason and noted he looked extremely pale. He looked as though he was about to pass out. 'Jason?' Declan said. 'Can you get some shoes for Elizabeth, please?'

'Yeah. Yeah, OK. Good thinking.' Jason headed out eagerly, glad to be doing something.

'Ready to wrap?' Declan asked Claire.

'All ready.'

'Do you need some towels to dry her arm?' Brett asked as they prepared to remove Elizabeth's arm from beneath the running water.

'No. We just leave it as it is and wrap it up,' Declan answered.

'Why plastic wrap?' Brett was totally confused.

'It stops the air getting to it. We've cooled the affected area quite considerably, which should hopefully minimise the depth of the burn.' Declan and Claire finished wrapping Elizabeth's arm and applied ice packs to reduce the amount of blistering.

'It hurts,' Elizabeth complained.

'I know,' Declan said, and Claire immediately began rummaging in one of the cupboards. She handed Elizabeth some paracetamol and gave her a small drink.

'I'm thirsty.'

'I know you are, darling,' Claire said, and kissed her sister's head. 'We'll deal with that at the hospital.'

'Let's get her to the car. I'll drive,' Declan said, taking his car keys from his pocket. Claire wasn't going to argue and instead she manoeuvred her sister into the back seat of his car and sat next to her.

'Lie down and elevate your legs,' Claire told Elizabeth. 'We need to keep your heart rate steady.' Once they had Elizabeth in position, Mary fixed a blanket over her and met Claire's gaze. The two sisters communicated without the need for any words.

'I'm coming, too,' Brett said, and received no argument from either of them. Declan understood. He knew how much Brett needed to be needed at this point of his life. He knew there was nothing he could do at the hospital that would make a difference but just being there would make him feel as though he was doing something.

'Good. Come and sit in the front and make sure I'm going the right way. OK. Let's go.' Declan climbed into the driver's seat and started the engine. At least Claire was able to monitor Elizabeth's condition. 'How's she doing?' he asked as he turned onto the main road into Mt Black.

'Holding her own. Aren't you, Lizzie?' Claire smoothed her sister's hair out of her eyes and pressed a kiss to her forehead. 'You'll be fine. Close your eyes, darling. I'm here. I'll look after you.' It didn't matter that Elizabeth was a grown woman of twenty-three and that Claire was only six years her senior. It was Claire's job to look after her family.

Elizabeth did as she was told and as Declan glanced at the two sisters in the back he recognised the bond of love. It was touching and sad at the same time. It was obvious the rest of her siblings looked up to her and right now Claire was in the role of mother, rather than sister. He felt for Claire, for the experiences she would have forgone due to her acceleration into a parental figure. He'd wished for so long for siblings, and when the twins had been born, he couldn't have been happier, but for all intents and purposes he'd been raised an only child. With sixteen years between himself and his siblings, he still felt closer to his parents in age. In fact, there was only eighteen years between himself and his mother. Not that he didn't love Helen and Evan, he did, with all the love a big brother could bestow, but it wasn't the same as what he'd witnessed Claire sharing with her family.

Now she was torn. Torn between being the sister, the mother and the doctor. Claire deserved to be the big sister, helping Elizabeth through the trauma, rather than being forced to treat the burns in a general and sometimes dispassionate manner, which their jobs called for.

'Which way now, Brett?' he asked as they came to a fork in the road.

'Left. Then take the second street on the right.'

Declan nodded and followed the instructions. 'How are you holding up?' he asked quietly.

Brett shrugged. 'Just worried about Lizzie.'

'I know.' He paused. 'Feel as though you have knots in your stomach?'

'Yeah. You sure she'll be OK?'

'Yes. I've seen patients recover from burns far worse than Elizabeth's. It'll take time but she'll make a full recovery.'

'Good. Kind of puts my own problems into perspective, but I just know I'm gonna fail that exam tomorrow.'

'You'll be fine. Just relax, focus on positive thoughts and calmly remember the things we covered tonight. Don't worry about anyone else in the room—do that afterwards.' Declan smiled and Brett had the grace to blush, knowing Declan was referring to Courtney. Brett smiled shyly and Declan was glad to see him relaxing a little. Good. The kid needed reassurance.

Having often dealt with trauma, Declan had often observed that, especially in a close family situation such as this, it tended to be more difficult for the bystanders than the patient. He checked his rear-vision mirror again and as they drove beneath the street lights, he noted the stress and worry on Claire's face as she held her sister.

When they arrived at the hospital, Declan parked in the ambulance bay—behind the ambulance—to facilitate an easy transition for Elizabeth.

'What do we do?' Brett asked, the anxiety back. 'Do we need to get her a wheelchair? A bed on wheels?'

'How are you feeling, Lizzie?' Claire asked softly. 'Feel as though you can walk?'

'Sure.' Elizabeth opened her eyes and nodded. 'Nothing wrong with my legs, right?'

Claire smiled and Declan saw some of the concern leave her. 'Come on. Let's get you inside.'

As they walked in, they were met by the night sister and the GP on call. 'Hi, Poncho.' Claire called as she led Elizabeth into a treatment room. Declan looked at Poncho and decided there was no way he was going to let this doctor look after Elizabeth.

The man was about five feet six, had dark grey hair and looked to be about seventy years old. Both hands were clasped together, mainly because one couldn't stop shaking. Declan diagnosed mild Parkinson's disease and wondered why the doctor was still on the GP rotation. How was he supposed to care for Elizabeth's delicate condition if he couldn't stop his own body from involuntary tremors?

Declan met Claire's gaze above the other doctor's head. She looked tired and exhausted. As far as he was concerned, he'd been the initial treating doctor and he intended for it to stay that way.

'Hi. Poncho, is it?' He held out his hand to the other doctor. 'I'm Declan Silvermark. The new ENT here. I'll be admitting Elizabeth and as I've already started treatment, I'll just continue.' He heard Claire sigh behind him and realised he'd just made the right decision.

'Replacing Dr Bean.' The old doctor nodded, then skewered Declan with a look so intense Declan decided he'd drastically underestimated his new colleague. 'You'd better treat the patients better than he did. The man was a liability.'

'Declan's very good,' Claire said with utter confidence.

'You stayed with him?' Poncho continued to study Declan.

'Yes.'

'So you know about burns, then, Dr ENT specialist?'

'I do, sir.'

'And you will look after our Claire's sister?'

'To the best of my ability, sir.' Declan held Poncho's gaze and obviously the doctor saw what he needed to see and finally looked away.

'All right.' Poncho turned to Claire. 'I'm sorry I'm not much help. An old fool like me.'

Claire smiled brightly. 'You're not an old fool.'

Declan shook his head, amazed at the way Claire captivated people. She was loved by this town. They got Elizabeth up onto the bed in the treatment room and Declan called Brett in. 'Come and talk to your sister. Tell her about your homework or what you're going to write for your exam paper tomorrow.'

'Aw, do I have to?'

'It'll help keep her mind occupied,' Declan said softly and Brett instantly caught on.

'Oh. Sure.'

'Great. He's going to bore me with Pythagoras' theorem.'

Elizabeth smiled tiredly as she spoke and Brett returned the gesture and was immediately relaxed.

'No. Actually, I'm going to bore you with Shakespeare—Othello—but if you want Pythagoras' theorem, I'll throw that in as an encore.' Brett grinned and Declan knew that one bit of teasing from his sister had reassured him more than anything anyone else could have said. Declan was glad Brett's anxiety regarding this situation seemed to be under control because Claire didn't need any more stress in her life tonight.

Declan cleared his throat. 'Did you want the nurse to contact Mary?'

'Yes.' Claire looked at him thankfully. 'I would have remembered later.'

He smiled. 'I understand. You're mind is preoccupied at the moment. Supplies are in the cupboards?'

Claire nodded, happy about him treating Elizabeth. 'Yes. I'll help you.'

'I'll watch closely,' Poncho said, giving Declan another glare. 'And I'll tell you if you are doing things wrong.'

'I'd appreciate that, sir.' Declan tried hard to hide his smile. 'All right. Are we ready to begin?'

'Is that my cue?' Brett asked, and cleared his throat. '*Othello*. A play by Shakespeare. The main characters are Othello, of course, and the fair Desdemona.'

'They were all fair.' Elizabeth sighed. 'Did Shakespeare ever write about any woman who he didn't classify as a fair maiden?'

Brett began to answer her question and Claire smiled, although she was a little puzzled. Usually, situations like this had Brett totally stressed out and she'd already planned to be up half the night with him yet again, helping him deal with his troubled thoughts. She would have made him stay back at the house to keep him out of the way but Declan had called the shots and she'd been too concerned with Elizabeth to contradict him. Now, though, Brett seemed to be dealing well with what was happening.

Declan had pulled on a protective gown and gloves and Claire did the same. When they were ready, they carefully unwrapped the plastic wrap from Elizabeth's arm and took a good look at the burn. Declan nodded. 'Looks to be border-line second degree. It could have been worse. You're a lucky girl, Elizabeth.' The nurse came in to help them out and Declan ordered lactacted Ringer's solution to help replace fluids as well as keep Elizabeth's electrolyte levels in check, thus hopefully stopping her from going into shock. Although she was joking with her brother, that was no indication of whether or not her body was coping with what had happened.

'I'm going to administer a local anaesthetic to the arm so we can debride the wound and see what we've got,' Declan said as he gave Elizabeth something for the pain. Claire actually administered the local anaesthetic and once it was doing its job, they could begin.

The skin had already started to blister and was a mottled white-pinkish colour and, before they'd administered the local, hypersensitive to touch. It was only because part of her top had become fused with her skin that he really needed to debride the area and once he was done and had managed to removed the fragments, they wrapped her arm in a proper burns dressing.

'You've been quiet, Poncho,' Claire said.

'He's a good doctor.' Poncho addressed his comment to Claire, completely ignoring Declan. 'Can we get him to stay on?'

'One step at a time.' Claire glanced at Declan, a teasing glint in her eyes. 'He's only had one day here. Let's see if we can talk him into a permanent contract after he's been here at least one week.'

'Hmm,' was all Declan said. Was that what the area was after? More doctors? He was an ENT specialist and although he'd enjoyed the general clinic today, treating different ailments, he was under contract with a hospital in Brisbane and was due to return there at the end of the week. 'How are you feeling, Elizabeth?'

'Mellow,' she replied, her head back and eyes closed.

'Brett?' Declan looked at the young man.

'Is she all done?'

'She's all done,' Declan answered. 'Told you she'd be fine.'

'Yeah. You were right, Dec.' Brett nodded and as Claire intercepted the gaze her youngest brother gave Declan, she recognised a bit of hero-worship going on. Oh, no. Brett was becoming attached to him and far too quickly. It had happened before with Ken, and when she and Ken had broken up, Brett had been devastated. Then again, he'd only been eleven at the time. Now, she hoped, being almost eighteen, he'd be able to deal with the fact that Declan wouldn't be a permanent fixture in their lives.

'So I can go home?' Elizabeth asked wistfully.

'Yes.' Claire sighed. 'Let's all go home.'

'She doesn't have to stay overnight?' Brett asked Declan, and Claire was once more struck by the way Brett was turning to this relative stranger rather than his own sister. It appeared Declan's charm worked on everyone—patients, siblings and, of course, herself—much to her chagrin.

'I think Elizabeth will sleep better in her own bed and no doubt Claire will be up every half-hour at least to check on her.'

Brett chuckled. 'You know our Claire.' He placed his arm around his big sister's shoulders. 'Always lookin' after us.'

'Come on, Brett. Let's leave Claire to help Elizabeth and go get the car ready.'

'You need to sign some papers first,' Poncho said.

'Right.' Declan nodded, then turned to smile at Claire, wondering why she stood there frowning at him.

The three left and Claire looked at her sister again. 'Let's get going.' Tiredness swamped her and she wished now she'd thought to have Jason drive one of their cars to the hospital so they didn't need to rely on Declan to take them back. She helped Elizabeth off the bed, the arm now expertly bandaged and in a sling, before taking her out to the car.

Once Elizabeth was settled, Claire headed back inside and called through to Mary to let her know what was happening before picking up the supplies they'd need so she could change Elizabeth's dressing the next morning.

When they were finally settled in the car, Claire leaned her head back and closed her eyes. Brett was once more sitting in the front and Elizabeth was lying down, her head in Claire's lap again, her feet up on the window. Declan had put soft music on and it was enough to lull Claire almost to sleep. She recognised Chopin and let her mind flow with the soothing strains.

'Declan's wonderful,' Elizabeth said quietly, and Claire realised another sibling had bitten the dust. 'How old is he? Do you think he's too old for me?'

'That's the anaesthetic talking.'

Elizabeth frowned. 'Don't you like him, Claire?'

'I'm too tired to worry about it right now. I just want to go home, Lizzie.'

'Oh, yeah. Me, too.' When they finally arrived back at the house, Mary, Jason, Thomas and Greg greeted them.

'I made another dessert,' Jason announced, and they all sat down to freshly baked scones with jam and ice cream. 'No cream,' he said sheepishly.

'You didn't need to go to all this trouble,' Claire said, but she helped herself to another one.

'Yes, I did. I needed to keep busy.' He kissed Elizabeth's head and gently hugged her. 'You're exhausted, Lizzie.'

Claire sighed. 'I guess I'd better get you into bed, our Liz.'

'I'll do it,' Jason said, and Claire gladly left him to look after his twin.

Declan stood. 'I'd better get going.'

Mary walked over and gave him a hug. 'Thank you, Declan. For everything.'

He smiled. 'No problem.'

Claire witnessed another one of her siblings falling under the charm of the new ENT and stood. 'I'll walk you to the car.'

'No. Please. It's cool outside.'

Claire grabbed a jacket from the coat rack. 'No problem.'

He said a general goodnight to everyone, wished Brett luck for his exam and headed outside, tired yet cautious and very aware of the woman by his side. 'It's been a hectic day.' Declan spoke softly.

'Yes.'

'Do you have a clinic early tomorrow morning?'

'No, but you do and I really should be there to introduce you to the patients.'

'It's not necessary, Claire. I'm sure I'll be able to muddle through. I have met patients on my own before.'

'Why are you doing this?' she blurted.

'Doing what?'

'Doing a clinic here in Mt Black.'

'Because the hospital needed an ENT specialist.' He frowned, not sure what she was getting at.

'But you could do anything. I've been watching you. You easily helped Brett with his homework, you were brilliant in clinic this afternoon and you treated Elizabeth's burns as though you were a burns specialist.'

'And?' He glanced over at her. 'That bothers you?'

'You did med school in three years, Declan.'

'We've covered this.'

'But you could have done anything. Neurosurgery. Cardiac surgery.'

'The brain and the heart are important but those jobs also come with a bucketload of stress. Besides, I preferred ENT.' He shrugged. 'Therefore, the choice was simple.'

'How old are you?'

'Thirty.'

'And how long have you been working in ENT?'

'Two years.'

'And what did you do with the other years in between?'

'Studied.'

'You're being coy. It doesn't suit you,' she growled tiredly.

'Why are you cross with me?'

'Because you could have done so much more with your life.'

'According to you. Don't you like *your* job?'

'Of course I do.'

'Yet you'd like to be more than just a GP?'

'I never said that.'

'No, but you're implying it with your questions.'

'Oh? Studied a bit of psychology as well, did you?'

'I've studied a lot of things. Look, Claire, it's no big deal. I like to study. I find it easy so naturally I've read up on a lot of different specialities. I still do. There's always something new to learn and although I love doing ENT work, that doesn't mean

I want to stop learning. Yes, I have a high IQ but it comes with a down side.'

'Really? And that is what? Being labelled a know-it-all?'

'Anxiety.' He said the word softly. 'I've had it all my life and I've had to learn how to deal with it. Sometimes it works. Sometimes it doesn't.'

'Anxiety?' It was the last thing she'd expected him to say.

'Yes. I'm not perfect and neither do I claim to be. I have faults, like everyone else in the world.'

'Really? I haven't seen any so far.' Apart from giving off mixed signals, and she still wasn't sure why she was so concerned about that.

'I can't paint.'

'Of course you can. Anyone can paint.'

Declan chuckled softly. 'No, they can't, Claire. I'm not an…instinctively creative person. The thought of doing some craft activity puts me into a spin. Those people who sit down and make cards and scrapbooks and curtains and clothes. Any sort of craft. I'm in awe of those people.'

'It's not that hard.' Her tone had calmed down and she leaned against his car.

'For you, perhaps. My mum likes to make scrapbooks and just watching her gives me a headache. When I was a teenager, she tried to get me to design a pattern. It didn't work. I can copy a drawing from a book, I can follow instructions to the letter but to creatively design something…like your abstract painting…' He shuddered. 'I can interpret it but I don't understand how you did it in the first place.'

'But that's just painting what you feel.'

'Exactly.'

'Are you saying you don't feel?'

'Of course I do, but I can't express it with a drawing. Designing a pattern—doodling, for want of a better word—gives me anxiety. More so than bungee-jumping.'

'You've done it?'

Declan laughed. 'It was one of the first things I did with my dad when he came back into my life. He showed me how to unwind, to relax. We now play golf together once a week and it's about the only down time my mind gets.'

'You said your parents are doctors.'

'That's right.'

'So you and your dad don't talk about work?'

'No. He forbids it. The golf course is medical-free…unless someone gets hit with a golf ball and knocked unconscious.'

'And I suppose that's happened.'

Declan laughed. 'Once or twice.'

'I guess you won't be playing golf with your dad this week.'

'We're playing on Saturday.'

'Of course. You finish your week here on Friday afternoon.'

'Gives me plenty of time to drive to the Gold Coast,' he agreed with a nod. 'It's only four hours from here.'

'We have a golf course here in Mt Black,' she felt compelled to point out. 'So if you need to relax during the week, you can always play there.'

'Thanks. Brett mentioned it but I've read the brochure at the motel which tells me all the wonderful sites of Mt Black. I probably won't get to explore much on this visit but I'm making a list.'

'Checking it twice?'

Declan smiled. 'I need to find out who's naughty and nice.' He, too, leaned against the car but he turned side on to face her. 'I hope both Elizabeth and Brett sleep well tonight. They should do.'

'I'm not so sure. I'll keep Elizabeth's medication up so she should be fine but Brett…' She trailed off and shook her head.

'He was the reason you were late this morning, wasn't he?'

She straightened and looked at him. 'How did you know?'

Declan shrugged. 'He's anxious about his exam. It's normal for him not to sleep.'

'He's not anxious. He's just stressed.'

Now was not the time, Declan realised. They were both tired and Claire needed to be in the right frame of mind to accept the truth about her brother. 'Well, he'll sleep OK tonight.'

Claire was immediately irritated at being told what her brother would or wouldn't do. 'How would you know, Declan? You hardly know him.'

Declan smiled curiously. 'That bothers you, doesn't it? Brett's a good kid. I see a lot of me in him.'

'Should I be worried, then?'

'I turned out all right.'

'So next I suppose you're going to tell me you know how he thinks?'

'Actually, yes. Besides, we have the anxiety thing in common.'

'What? Anxiety? Brett doesn't have anxiety.' But even as she said the words, it was as though penny after penny began to drop. The stress, the inability to cope with change, the pressure of his current workload, being unable to sleep... 'Oh, my gosh. He has anxiety!' She thought about him wanting to leave and go to uni on the Gold Coast. 'No, he doesn't.' She shook her head.

'We don't need to get into this now. It's late. You're tired. I'm tired. I'll see you tomorrow.' Declan took out his keys and jangled them. She didn't move and as she was leaning against the driver's door, that made it a little difficult for him to follow through.

'I'm very protective of my family,' she said at last.

'You have every right to be. They're all amazing people.'

'I know but I don't know if it's a good idea for you to get involved with them.'

Obviously she had something she wanted to say to him. It didn't matter one way or the other. Tired or not, there wasn't much chance of him getting any sleep tonight because he knew his thoughts would be plagued by a beguiling blond-haired, brown-eyed beauty. 'Go on.'

'It's just that Brett is already attaching himself to you and Elizabeth wants to date you and—'

'Whoa. Whoa. Time out.' He made the 'T' sign with his hands. 'You're getting agitated over something that's really very simple.' He placed his hands on her shoulders and looked at her.

'What's that?'

'I like your family.'

'I know.'

'They're easy to like. They're very likeable people.' He slowly slid his hands up and down her arms, warming them but drawing her closer. 'And so are you. *Very* likeable.' He did something then that he'd wanted to do since first seeing her hair flowing loosely about her shoulders. He ran his fingers through the soft, silky strands. 'Gorgeous,' he said, more to himself than her, but the single word made Claire's stomach swim with butterflies.

Part of her wanted to go to him, to be wrapped in his arms, with his mouth on hers, and to forget herself, even if it was for just a moment. The other part, the sensible part, wanted to put as much distance between them as possible.

'Declan. Don't.' The word was soft, whispered and half pleading, half encouraging as she rubbed her cheek against the palm of his hand.

Declan tilted her face upwards and lowered his mouth to brush her lips lightly with his. 'I don't mean to confuse you, Claire. Honestly, I don't, but there's something between us. I have no idea what it is but I do think it's worth attempting to find out. This is new territory for me as well. It's hard for a person with anxiety to be spontaneous, but I'm working on it.'

'Well, I'd say you're doing a good job.'

He smiled and rubbed her arms once more. 'Thanks.' He paused. 'You should go inside. It's cold.'

She nodded but realised she didn't want to move. She wanted to prolong her time alone with him but knew he was right. 'Are you sure Brett will sleep well tonight?'

'Almost positive. We've had a few chats and I've managed to lower his anxiety levels. That always helps.'

'So who's going to help lower your anxiety levels?'

'You think I'm anxious?' She was one hundred per cent correct but he was surprised she knew that.

'Yes. Because of this.' Without another thought Claire stepped forward and pressed her mouth firmly to his. His gasp of shocked delight was enough to thrill her to her toes. It only took a moment for his arms to fold around her, moulding her body to his as he reciprocated her touch.

She felt incredible. He couldn't believe how right she felt in his arms, and where he'd been more than content to take anything between them at a snail's pace, here she was, rushing him... And he was enjoying every moment of it. So unusual, so thought-provoking, so enticing.

As suddenly as the embrace had started she broke away and took two huge steps backwards out of reach. 'Sleep well, Declan.'

'Yeah, right,' she heard him mutter as she entered the house, a smile on her face and a spring in her step.

CHAPTER FIVE

WHEN CLAIRE ARRIVED at the hospital the next morning, she was surprised to find Declan sitting at the nurse's desk, writing notes.

'What are you doing here so early?' she asked as she stowed her bag.

He glanced up, checked his watch and then smiled at her. 'I've been here for a while. Night Sister let me through to the clinic.' He indicated the case files in front of him. 'Thought I'd at least take the opportunity to read the patient notes before I see everyone. Besides, I thought I told you not to bother coming in this morning.'

Claire shrugged and headed towards the kitchen. 'Habit,' she called over her shoulder. She made a cup of coffee, deep in thought. The instant she'd seen him at the desk, she'd felt her body begin to tremble. Of course she'd known she would see him that morning but she hadn't expected it to be first thing and therefore hadn't been as prepared as she'd hoped. The man just had to look at her and she tingled all over. It wasn't right. It wasn't the way she wanted to live her life but, regardless of what she wanted, she was attracted to him and at the moment she thought it was better to simply go with it rather than fight it. Or, at least, that was what she was telling herself.

Besides, he was only here for the week then he would go away and she'd have a full three weeks to get herself under control before he returned. Mary had called her this morning, mainly to check on Elizabeth, but her sister had told her to just enjoy the flirting, the *double entendres* and to accept Declan's delicious smiles. Claire hadn't had the guts to tell Mary that she'd already kissed Declan—twice. That was something she needed to keep to herself, at least until she figured out what it meant.

She was the type of woman who liked to be in control. She handled things as they were thrown at her and at the moment this was the only way she could handle Declan and the attraction she had to him. Her siblings were always telling her to let go, to let loose, to do something wild and different, but in all honesty she wasn't that sort of woman. She liked things to be the same, to have the comfort of the familiar, and although Declan's presence in her life was starting to raise questions, they were still nothing to do with him. She would figure out what this attraction meant and she would figure out how to deal with it.

With a firm nod of confidence she felt as though she was back in control once more. She stirred her coffee one last time before taking a deep breath, squaring her shoulders and heading back out to where he would still be reading and writing. She admired his dedication and was pleased the hospital board had appointed a doctor of his calibre. Hopefully, now the patients requiring ear, nose and throat specialist care would receive it from a decent doctor rather than the farce that had been Dr Bean.

'How's Elizabeth?' Declan asked as soon as she returned from the kitchen.

'Much better this morning.' She sat in the chair next to him. 'Her arm's still red but not as bad as it was last night.'

'Good.' He put his pen down and looked at her. 'And Brett? Did he sleep all right?'

Claire smiled, loving the way he gave her his full attention. 'Yes, he did.'

'Told you.'

'Yeah, you did. You called it. You knew what was going to happen. You're the genius, Dr Silvermark.'

He grinned at her teasing. 'Thank you, thank you.'

'In fact, Jason mentioned this morning that maybe you'd like to come to dinner tonight as well—you know, so we can all properly thank you for taking care of Elizabeth.' Claire tried to make the invitation sound as though it was a common occurrence for her to ask a man over. Of course, she'd have to share him with her family again but she'd decided on the drive to work that morning that she wasn't going to let that bother her. In fact, wasn't it a good thing he was interested in getting to know them? It would help him to settle into his rotations here in Mt Black with ease. That way, whenever he came to town, he knew more than just the hospital staff.

'I don't want you to feel pressured to ask me around, Claire.'

'I'm not,' she said defensively. 'Besides, Jason is Elizabeth's twin and so he feels more responsible for her and therefore he wants to thank you again.'

'I see.' He remembered her words from last night. 'So you're not worried about me getting to know your siblings now?'

She paused, still not used to his direct honesty. She finally decided the best way to answer him was in the same vein. 'I don't know.'

He chuckled. 'That's surprising.'

'It is? How?'

'Well, you always seem so in control. Hardly anything fazes you. You have an inner strength, Claire, and I admire that.'

'Thank you.' She was flattered by his words, by his charm, by the way he was smiling at her. 'Well, I admire your confidence.'

He raised his eyebrows at that and she continued.

'I mean, with your work. You know exactly what you're doing and how to do it and your mind picks up things normal people wouldn't pick up and…' She was babbling. The man had her entering areas she'd never thought she'd enter and this was one of them. Babbling! She *never* babbled, yet here she was… babbling. She forced herself to stop and closed her mouth. 'Sorry.'

'Hey. Don't stop. What man doesn't want to hear a woman sing his virtues?'

'I wasn't singing.'

'You know what I mean.' He watched her for a moment, pleased to see her a little flustered. It was nice to know he affected her in such a way, just as she affected him. 'My confidence would have to come from my parents. They've always told me to stand firm in my convictions. When something feels right, that's usually an indication to pursue that path.'

Claire swallowed and blinked before asking, 'And what path are you following now?' Was that her voice sounding so husky? She was openly flirting with him—and she was having fun.

'The one you're standing on,' he replied, and she was pleased to hear his tone deepen, indicating he was just as affected by what was going on as she was. 'I'm attracted to you, Claire. Whether or not it's prudent to explore that attraction remains to be seen.'

That stunned her. 'I thought...I mean, last night, you seemed...' She trailed off, not sure what she was trying to say.

'Seemed eager? I am eager but, as I said, it's difficult for a person with anxiety to be spontaneous. I tend to over-think things. My father says it's my biggest failing and that I should learn to act on impulse more often.'

'I'd say you were very impulsive yesterday...' Claire began to blush a little. 'Well, a few times, at least.'

Declan laughed again and nodded. 'You didn't do too badly yourself, especially just before you went inside the house.'

'Oh, my.' Claire placed a hand on her cheek and looked away, surprised at how embarrassed she was. 'Should we be talking about this?'

'About the way you threw your arms around me and kissed me with abandon?'

She met his gaze, glaring at him. 'Yes.'

He shrugged. 'Sure. Why not?' He leaned a little closer and she breathed in his mesmerising scent. 'Fancy a repeat?'

'Yes. No,' she added quickly. She needed to get herself together. 'Look, Declan, if we're going to work together, we need to have some rules.'

'Rules.' He sat back in his seat and cleared his throat, but his gaze didn't leave her lips and she felt as though he'd once more brushed his mouth across hers in that same tantalising way he'd done last night. 'I love rules. I live by rules. Let's have 'em.'

'Well...um...'

'That's an interesting start. Not sure what it means, but I guess it could mean this.' He leaned over and pressed his lips to her cheek. 'That could be "well".' His voice had dropped to a whisper and he closed his eyes as he breathed in the tantalising scent of her. Dipping his head, he brushed his cheek softly against hers, his lips hovering near her neck, a neck he was becoming desperate to nuzzle. 'This could be "um".'

As he spoke his breath fanned her neck, causing goose-bumps to cascade down one side of her body. She shivered. It was wrong, so very wrong for him to be so enticing this early in the morning. Claire had come to work in the hope she'd be able to give her mind something else to focus on, such as hospital stress. She'd dreamt about him last night. He'd been her first waking thought that morning and now here he was, once more wreaking havoc with her emotions…emotions she was too scared to feel in case they overpowered her and made her lose all self-control.

'Claire,' he murmured, his lips pressing tiny butterfly kisses to her neck and around to her ear.

'Mmm?' Her eyes were closed and her head was tilted to the side, allowing him all the access he wanted.

'Any other rules you want to think up?'

She smiled dreamily and sighed.

'I like that rule,' he said in response to her sigh. Slowly, he lifted his head and pulled back a little. Claire opened her eyes and met his gaze. 'Seriously, though, I'm not sure if I can stop wanting to kiss you.'

'It's all happening so fast,' she whispered.

'I know.'

'We hardly know each other.'

Declan nodded and shifted further back. 'Then I suggest we get to know each other better.'

'And cool the touchy-feely parts.' Claire looked at his lips, her tongue coming out to wet her own.

'Is that a question?'

Claire's gaze flicked back to his and Declan smiled, the effect going straight to her already churning stomach.

'Or a statement?' He reached out and took her hand in his. Her skin was so smooth and delicate he felt if he didn't handle her with kid gloves, she'd break. 'How about we not make a decision on that? At least, not yet. We both seem to like the kissing parts.'

Claire could feel herself beginning to blush again and momentarily glanced down at their entwined fingers.

'If either one of us thinks it's moving way too fast, then we be honest. That's what we're doing now. Being honest.'

Claire smiled. 'Really? It sounds more like psychoanalysing.'

Declan chuckled and nodded. 'It is. I told you I tend to over-think things. I need to work through things so I can understand what's going on in my head.' He shrugged. 'It's hard to break a habit of a lifetime.'

'You only need to break bad habits, Declan.'

'Exactly, and kissing you could definitely become a good habit so there's no need to break it. Right?'

'Are you teasing me now?'

His smile broadened. 'And if I am?'

Claire extracted her fingers from his and stood. 'Then I think you'd better stop.'

'Why?'

'Because it flusters me.'

'I know.' His smile broadened. 'I like that.'

Claire shook her head and frowned. 'You know, yesterday morning I wasn't even sure I liked you.'

'And now?'

She rolled her eyes and crossed her arms over her chest. 'Declan.'

'Yes?'

'Do you intend to be serious?'

His blue gaze deepened. 'I'm being *very* serious, Claire.'

Once more her body responded with tingles and goose-bumps and this time he was nowhere near as close as he'd been before. How could he affect her so wildly just by looking at her? 'I don't even know how this conversation started.'

'You asked me to dinner.'

She sighed. 'So I did. Do you want to come?'

'Depends on what time. I have an appointment later this afternoon.'

'Oh.' Claire was surprised. She had thought he didn't know

anyone in Mt Black—at least, that's the impression he'd given. 'Patient?'

'Not exactly.'

'Well…um…'

'Are you sure you want to say "well…um"?' He stood and edged closer. 'Remember the new rules?'

'Declan.' Claire put a hand up to his chest to hold him off but instead felt the instant warmth of his skin beneath his shirt. She swallowed, her gaze flicking down to her hand before coming back to meet his gaze. She saw the spark of desire there and quickly removed her hand, as though burnt. She moved backwards, hitting her leg on the side of the desk. 'Ow.'

'You all right?' He was instantly concerned. Claire glowered at him.

'I'm fine.' She rubbed her leg where she'd hit it. 'If you're not free, Jason's just going to have to learn to live with it.'

'If you don't mind me coming a little later—say around seven?'

'Should be fine.'

'Good. I'll look forward to it. Jason is a good chef.'

'Yes.' There was pride in the word. 'All right. Seven o'clock it is. Do you remember the way?'

'I think so. I can always ask for directions if I get lost.'

'No.' The word came quickly from her mouth. If he did that, if he got lost and asked one of the locals where she lived, they might think there was something going on between them, and that would never do. She'd lived through enough town gossip and she could do without more. Declan was merely a colleague—one she was attracted to, but that was no one's business but hers. Besides, when he left at the end of the week, her life would return to normal and she could do without any innuendos or speculation being tossed around. 'If you get lost, call me on my cell phone and I'll give you directions.'

Declan nodded. 'I'll do that.'

'Good.' She picked up the list of patients she'd be seeing that afternoon and went to the file compactors which were located to the side of the desk. She concentrated on pulling the files, getting things organised for her clinic. After a minute or two she glanced across to where Declan had seated himself again and was once more going through the remainder of the casenotes.

'Claire,' he said, and she immediately turned her head away from him in case he caught her staring at him.

'Yes?' She stayed where she was.

'What can you tell me about Mr Peterson?'

'Dwight Peterson?' Claire walked over. 'He's deaf in his left ear and complained about five weeks ago of a painful right ear. I had a look and the ear was severely inflamed with discharge in the ear canal. I wasn't sure whether it was just otitis media or something else like that.'

'So you referred him on?'

'Yes. He saw Dr Bean at the last ENT clinic. Why?'

'Dr Bean hasn't prescribed any follow-up. In fact, the man hardly wrote any notes whatsoever, and those he did write are almost illegible. Generally, if you're planning to see a patient again or want them to have follow-up treatment, you make a note of it.'

Claire frowned. 'So what's the problem? Isn't Mr Peterson coming in today?'

'No. I've finished the notes for today's clinic and thought I'd go through the notes of the previous ENT clinic. Yesterday I picked up quite a few problems and thought there might be more. I still want to go through the paed clinic from last month and hopefully I'll get around to that some time this afternoon or tomorrow. When do I have house calls?'

'Tomorrow. What do you want to do about Mr Peterson?'

'I'd like you to get him in to see me a.s.a.p. I don't care when or where I see him but I want him seen today. Dr Bean has noted the patient had a sore back and that combined with an ear infection could be something other than severe otitis media. When a patient already has a pre-existing disability—and in Mr Peterson's case it's loss of hearing in his left ear—it's imperative to tread carefully and guard the remaining sensory modality.'

'Give me the notes. I'll call his house.'

Declan checked the clock. 'It's almost eight. Is that too early to call?'

'No. He's a dairy farmer.'

'Then by all means.' He indicated the phone. Claire took the file from him and picked up the receiver. After dialling the number she waited for it to be connected but there was no answer.

'That's odd.'

'What? No answer?' Declan's voice was cautious.

'No.'

'I have a bad feeling about this.'

'So do I.' She disconnected the call and dialled another number.

'Who are you calling now?'

'Frankie. He's in charge of our police station. I'll get him to send someone out to check on Dwight and his wife.'

'Good.' The clinic door opened and Bethany walked in, surprised to find both doctors there already.

'Getting an early start?'

'Something like that,' Declan grumbled, and stood, gathering up the files. 'I'll give you back your desk.'

'You're all right,' Bethany said, but Declan merely smiled and took the files into one of the clinic rooms. 'He's not in a good mood?' Bethany whispered to Claire.

'He has reason. Looks as though Dr Bean's stuffed up again.' Her call was connected and she spoke into the receiver, giving Frankie the details. After she'd hung up, Bethany raised her eyebrows.

'Something wrong with Dwight?'

'Not sure. I guess we'll find out…when we find Dwight, that is.' The clinic door opened again and this time Declan's first patient came in. 'I'll let him know we're ready to start.' She went into the first clinic room.

'Any luck?' he asked, not looking up from what he was reading.

'Frankie's going to send someone round.'

'Good. He'll let us know what transpires?'

'Yes. I've asked him to keep in close contact.' Claire stood where she was for a moment and Declan looked up.

'First patient's here?'

'Yes.' Still she didn't move.

'Something else wrong?'

'How did you know to check the notes?'

'I told you. After what I saw yesterday, I wanted to make sure there weren't any other patients who had slipped through the slippery fingers of Dr Bean.'

'Dwight could be in a serious condition.'

'Or he could just be out milking the cows and as right as rain. Dr Bean prescribed antibiotics and if it was otitis media, it would have cleared it up.'

'I doubt it,' Claire said softly.

Declan met her gaze. 'So do I.'

The sound of the clinic door opening yet again broke the moment. 'Clinic time,' Declan murmured.

'Yes. I'll start checking into every patient who's seen Dr Bean.'

'That'll take a while.'

'Then let's hope we can get through this before the end of your first week here.'

Declan smiled. 'A workaholic. A woman after my own heart.' As he said the innocent words, he realised she might misconstrue them. 'I didn't mean anything by that,' he said haltingly.

She nodded. 'I know.' With that, she turned on her heel and left. Declan watched her go and wondered what it was that was holding her back. She'd told him she didn't want a relationship, that she was happy with her life the way it was, that she was looking forward to peace and solitude, but he already knew someone like Claire needed close friends around her. Not many but a few very close friends. Did he want to be one of those? The instant answer was yes but it also brought with it a lot of questions and insecurities.

He was thirty years old but he hadn't had many girlfriends during his life and the ones he had dated had all been long term. Still, he'd never felt such an instant attraction with any of them, the way he did with Claire. She was something special, different, and he definitely wanted more. It was all so strange but, like his dad had taught him, when something felt right, go with it. That gut instinct had got him through a lot of situations and he'd learned to trust it. He had a gut instinct about Dwight Peterson, that something was wrong, and he was following that instinct.

Was it safe to follow his instincts where Claire was concerned?

It was definitely something to ponder at a later time but right now if he didn't start his clinic, he'd end up running late and with so many files to read, that was the last thing he wanted. Organising his desk, he consulted his patient list and pulled out the correct file before going and calling his first patient through.

The clinic ran smoothly, with Claire introducing him to most of the patients just before he ushered them into the consulting room. Every time he went into the waiting room to get the next patient, he noticed the pile of casenotes Claire and Bethany were pulling kept growing and growing.

'Any news on Mr Peterson?' he asked, keeping his voice low. 'It's been over an hour since you called the police.'

Claire shook her head. 'Nothing concrete. Frankie sent someone out to their dairy farm but only found the milkers.'

'The whatters?'

'The Petersons employ two young men to help out with the milking. Dwight's getting on in years. Anyway, they said Dwight hadn't turned up for milking last night, and this morning they hadn't seen either him or his wife.'

'I don't like this.'

Claire agreed. 'Frankie reported Dwight's car wasn't there so they're out looking for it now. It wasn't on the main road to Mt Black so we'll just have to wait.'

'Please, interrupt me the instant you hear anything.'

'Will do.'

Declan called his next patient through and had started his examination when Bethany came rushing into the room. 'Claire needs you in Emergency.'

Declan was on his feet instantly. 'They've found Dwight?'

'Yes. He's not in a good way.'

Leaving Bethany to explain to his clinic patients, Declan headed through the door to Accident and Emergency. He could see Claire outside the hospital with one of the nurses and a barouche bed, the red and blue flashing lights of the police car reflecting off the walls as they continued to spin around.

Declan went into the first treatment room and washed his

hands before pulling on protective gown and gloves. Claire met his gaze as the bed was wheeled in and the look on her face told him to expect something serious.

Declan took one look at Dwight Peterson and the severe swelling around the right side of the neck and realised he wouldn't be returning to his clinic that afternoon. Mr Peterson would be needing emergency surgery.

CHAPTER SIX

'WHAT have we got?" Declan asked.

'Dwight Peterson,' she said. 'Eighty-two-year-old dairy farmer. Severe swelling of the right side of the neck. No known allergies.'

'Wife's name?' Declan's voice was quiet.

'Phyllis.'

'She's here?' While he spoke, he hooked the stethoscope into his ears and quickly listened to Dwight's heart.

'Yes. She was bringing him in to the hospital and he collapsed across her while she was driving, forcing the car off the road and into a tree.'

'Is she all right?'

'Bethany's going to look at her.'

Declan nodded again and glanced at the staff in the small treatment room. He had Claire and two nurses at his disposal and he doubted it would be enough. Just from a quick glance at Dwight and from what he'd learned, reading the notes, this wasn't going to be easy. At least Dwight's heart was still beating. Always a good sign.

'Pupils equal and reacting to light,' Claire announced.

'Good. Start him on IV fluids to combat dehydration and give him IV penicillin as well. I'll need a complete blood count and…' Declan trailed off, feeling Dwight's neck.

'And what?' Claire asked as she checked their patient's blood pressure.

'Temperature is thirty-nine degrees Celsius,' the nurse reported.

'I need him in Brisbane,' Declan muttered, his hands still on Dwight's neck. 'The swelling is extensive and his neck is resisting movement. I'll need to operate. Get Frankie to make a note of everyone Dwight's come into contact with during the last few days. Also, you may want to get a vet out to those cows.'

'Declan?' Claire gazed at him wide-eyed.

'I need him in Brisbane. He needs an MRI, CSF analysis, CBC and other tests. I can't wait for answers here. I need them immediately. What's his blood pressure?'

'One-eighty over one-ten.'

'It's clear he's vomited. Hook him up to the EEG, oximeter and double-glove, double-gown and mask procedures.'

'Declan?' Claire spread her hands wide.

'He may have meningitis,' Declan said softly.

'Meningitis? How can you be sure?'

'I can't. That's why I want him in Brisbane. He needs further testing and as I said, I'll definitely be operating. But if it *is* meningitis, it's better we take precautions now.' He angled his head towards the doorway. 'I'll stay here. You get the transfer organised.' Claire headed out of the treatment room. 'Oh Claire. Let Bethany know and give Phyllis prophylactic antibiotics. All staff will need to be treated as well.'

'How sure are you?'

'Ninety-five per cent.'

Claire nodded, deciding she needed to take his word for it. He was the specialist as well as the genius, so she set about doing what she'd been told.

When the helicopter landed on the roof at the hospital in Brisbane, it really was action stations. They were met by two of Declan's staff, both wearing masks to protect themselves. He'd called ahead to the hospital to get them to set up what he needed. The moment he alighted from the aircraft, Claire watched him change. Here he was, back in his habitat, and he was all business.

She hung back and helped Phyllis to safety from the chopper

blades. Declan looked around for her but she waved him away. 'I'll catch up,' she yelled. He frowned but nodded and left with his staff.

Once they were inside, Claire turned to Phyllis. 'You do realise that both you and Dwight will be in isolation. If Declan is right and Dwight does have meningitis, it needs to be controlled and contained as quickly as possible.'

Phyllis nodded. 'I just want him to be all right.'

Claire reassured her. 'Declan will do everything he can.'

'How did this happen, Claire? How did it come to this?'

Claire swallowed, knowing it was Dr Bean's fault that things had progressed so far, but she couldn't say it, wasn't allowed to say it. 'We can talk about that later. Now, though, let's find where they are and get you settled.' She took Phyllis's hand in hers. 'You're still shaking. Are you sure you're all right? You've had a scary morning.'

'He was up last night. Not feeling well. He kept saying his head was hurting so bad it was worse than any hangover he's ever had. First of all I thought he was just being funny but then he just seemed to get worse and he refused to let me drive him to the hospital.' Tears were cascading down her cheeks and Claire quickly pulled a tissue from her pocket.

A pretty brunette nurse came by and stopped. 'Can I help you?' she asked.

'Er…Declan Silvermark?' Claire said.

'Oh, Declan.' The nurse smiled. 'He's with a patient.'

'We came with him. This is the patient's wife.'

'Right. Then you can wait in the family waiting room.'

Claire felt like stamping her foot and having a tantrum. She lifted her chin defiantly and spoke in her best clinical voice. 'Dwight Peterson, the patient with Dr Silvermark, may have meningitis. This is his wife. I am his doctor. We may have both been exposed and would like somewhere else to wait, preferably in the isolation room with the patient, so as not to spread any unnecessary germs around the rest of the hospital.'

'Well. Quite the little spitfire, aren't you?' the nurse said, her demeanour changing.

Claire held her ground. She hated big hospitals. She hated the impersonality of them and the way miscommunication could easily get out of hand.

'You'd better come through here, then.' She indicated a door but the instant they went inside she made both Claire and Phyllis stop before handing them masks. The nurse put one on herself. 'This way,' she said once they were ready. She took them through to the isolation room where Claire could see Declan giving out orders. One of his team was taking a blood sample, another held out a clipboard with forms attached, which Declan scanned and then signed.

'There you go,' the nurse said.

'Thank you. Sorry I snapped earlier.'

The nurse shrugged. Claire urged Phyllis to go in and was about to go herself when she caught the nurse looking through the window at Declan and sighing. 'So you're the doctor who's taking our Declan away from us once a month.'

'Actually, he's employed by the hospital and until yesterday I had no idea who he was so I could hardly stand up to your accusation.'

The nurse smiled. 'No accusation, just…' She sighed again. 'Dreamy Declan. He's considered the hospital's most eligible bachelor.'

Claire raised her eyebrows, not really wanting to stay here and make chit-chat about Declan but interested to hear it anyway. 'How does he feel about that?'

'Declan?' She laughed. 'I think he hates it.'

That was the answer Claire would have come up with.

'He really keeps to himself, which is a shame because he's young, gorgeous and smart. What more does a woman want?' She laughed lightly. 'He doesn't socialise with any staff, always turns down drinks or dinner offers—from everyone, not just the females. It's quite strange but, still, the girls keep trying.'

'He likes his own space,' Claire muttered, but what the nurse was saying didn't match with his behaviour in Mt Black. Declan had been more than happy to have dinner at her house and to get involved with her family. Then again, with his anxiety being what it was, he probably wasn't too good in crowds. One on one would be much better. She swallowed at that thought. One on one? That's exactly what she'd had with him last night as well as this morning before clinic had begun and she had loved every moment of that one-on-one time.

'I guess he's keeping to himself in Mt Black, too. Hotel and hospital. That would be our Dec.' The nurse sighed dreamily once more and Claire shook her head.

'Well, it was nice chatting. I'd better get in there before he—'

'Claire!' It was Declan's voice but where was it coming from?

The nurse pointed up to the speaker outside the room. Claire looked at Declan inside the glass cubicle and saw that he had his elbow pressed to a speaker button. 'Are you planning to join me some time today? I need you.'

'Oops.' The nurse giggled. 'Now he's mad. It makes him even cuter, don't you think?'

Claire didn't want to think and instead started to focus her mind where it should have been—on helping Declan look after their patient. She quickly entered, walked directly to the sink and started washing her hands.

When she was ready, she walked over to Declan who handed her the otoscope. 'Have a look,' was all he said.

Claire did as she was told and was surprised at the amount of discharge coming from the ear. 'This is…'

'Very wrong.' He kept his words quiet, conscious of Phyllis's presence by her husband's side. 'He's about to go for his MRI and I have the path lab doing a rush on all his tests. We'll know more soon.'

Claire nodded and angled her head towards the wash sink, where they should be able to talk more privately. Once there, Declan stood close, *very* close, his hand on her elbow, his mouth not far from her ear. Claire wished he wouldn't. His nearness was creating havoc with emotions she was desperately trying to keep under control.

'They need to sue the hospital.'

Claire glanced up, meeting his gaze, but didn't speak.

'Dr Bean has been severely negligent. I could find no mention in the casenotes that he'd even examined Dwight using an otoscope, for crying out loud. ENTs are born with otoscopes as a sixth finger. How could he not have done that?'

'And if he had?'

'If he had, there's a high probability we wouldn't be here today with Dwight's hearing at risk. You know, Claire, as well as I do, that when a patient has a pre-existing disability you take extra care. Complete loss of a sensory modality is devastating. You saw Dwight and because of his symptoms referred him on. You did the right thing. You're in the clear but, Claire, Dwight presented with a troublesome ENT history and vertigo. That alone is enough for a specialist to actually do something about it, but the man didn't even look in the ear canal or at least he didn't note that in the casenotes.'

'So you can't say for sure?'

'Dwight says he didn't.'

'He's been able to talk?'

'Not much, but that was one of the questions I asked. He may not be remembering correctly or the pain may be making him say what he thinks I want to hear, but we can cross that bridge later when he's better. When we get back, we need to speak to Ken. The Petersons have every right to make a claim and they should also sue Dr Bean directly.'

'All right. All right.' She put her hand on his shoulder. 'Calm down.'

'Claire, due to the mistreatment, Dwight might die. It's highly probably he'll lose the hearing in his right ear, which will leave him totally deaf. All of this could have been prevented.'

'I realise that but it hasn't. Now breathe.' She took a breath in and let it out. 'Come on, join in.' It was strange and she smiled. 'I was doing this with Brett just the other night, trying to calm him down about school.'

Declan frowned.

'No, don't frown. Did you know that your brain can't tell the difference between a fake smile and a real smile? So if you force a smile, your body will release endorphins, thereby helping you to relax.'

Declan's frown deepened as she mimicked what he'd said to her yesterday. 'Well, at least you were listening,' he muttered.

It was then Claire became conscious that her hand was still on his shoulder and she immediately dropped it. 'We'll deal with Dwight and his treatment, one step at a time. First, let's see what the MRI shows.'

'You're right. So right, Claire.' He leaned even closer. 'And I can feel those endorphins working. Thanks.' He winked at her.

The orderly came into the room to take Dwight to Radiology for the MRI and Declan immediately stepped back, putting distance between himself and Claire. He was protective of her and didn't want her to be gossiped about. He knew there was plenty of gossip about him floating around and he did his best to ignore it, but he didn't want anyone gossiping about Claire.

She opted to go with Phyllis and Dwight while he had the MRI and Declan was glad for the distance. The woman drove him insane with wanting and that was a new sensation for him to be going through. Now was definitely not the time but he couldn't help it. The woman was interfering with his thoughts, both while he was awake but more especially when he was asleep. After the kiss she'd given him last night he'd hardly slept and now, when it looked like he could be in Theatre for a while, he wished he *had* managed to get more sleep than he had.

He decided work would be beneficial and headed to his office. Once there and after surprising the ENT department secretary, he set to work securing emergency theatre time for his patient. Once that was done, he contacted his cousin, Louisa, to see whether she could make it to Mt Black for a clinic on Friday.

'So what's it like?' Louisa asked.

'Mt Black? Not bad. Quaint. Lots of craft shops.'

'Your mum would love that,' Louisa pointed out.

'Yeah, but not your mum, though.'

Louisa laughed. 'You'd be surprised. A lot of bodyguards are taking up quilting. Mum says it relaxes her after protecting her clients all day long.'

Declan chuckled. 'Good ol' Aunt Melina. It was just as well Dad taught her how to defend herself at a young age.'

'Otherwise she had no idea what to do with her life. She was quite disappointed when I wanted to go in a completely different direction.'

'Taking care of people instead of beating them up?' Declan smiled.

'Something like that.'

'So you can make the clinic? I'm sorry it's such short notice, Lou.'

'You aren't sorry. Besides, if you can't take advantage of your family members, who can you take advantage of?'

Declan smiled. He could almost hear Claire saying something just like that. In fact, Louisa and Claire would get along really well.

'So, tell me, Declan. After a few days out in the quiet country town, did you like it?'

'Yes, actually. A lot better than the big hospital.'

'Still not settled in?'

'I doubt I'll ever be settled in here, Lou. They can't see past the novelty.'

'The young, smart doctor, eh?'

'Something like that.'

'So we're talking about a move to the sticks, or what?'

'To be honest, Lou, the thought has crossed my mind.'

Louisa laughed. 'Declan—everything crosses your mind. Such a busy mind you have.'

Declan joined in her laughter, There was a knock on his office door and he called for the person to enter. 'I've gotta go, Lou. I'll talk to you later.'

'Sure. See you on Friday, cuz.'

The door opened and Claire walked tentatively into the room. Declan beckoned her in as he replaced the receiver. 'Dwight back from Radiology?' He held out his hand for the packet of films she had. Claire handed them over without a word.

Declan flicked on the viewing box and hooked up one of the scans.

'It's not good,' she told him.

'I can see that. Any path results back yet?'

'I haven't checked with the nursing staff but I can, if you want.'

Declan swapped films, shaking his head and trying to control his anger. This could all have been avoided but, as Claire had pointed out, they just needed to take one step at a time. Now was not the time for anger, it was the time for healing—and it was up to him to put things right.

'Well, that certainly explains why he couldn't move his neck. Look at the size of it.'

'What is it, exactly?' Claire asked, gazing at the scans.

Declan pointed. 'There's extensive bony erosion of the mastoid. That'll need draining.'

'How do you do that?'

'Mastoidectomy. It's where I'll chisel off part of the surface bone of the mastoid...' he placed his fingers behind his ear, indicating the mastoid bone '...and release the pus. That will allow drainage. Once the bacterial meningitis is confirmed, I'll get Dwight started on a cocktail of antibiotics as well as codeine for the headaches and phenytoin to help prevent seizures, and he'll be on his way to a full recovery.'

'And his hearing?'

Declan shrugged. 'It depends how far the infection has spread.' He snapped his fingers. 'Darn. I should have asked Louisa to look in on Dwight.'

'The audiologist?'

'Yes.'

Claire pointed to the phone. 'That's who you were talking to?'

'Yes.'

She filed that away. For a guy who preferred to keep to himself, he'd been quite jovial on the phone when she'd walked into the room. 'You've worked with Louisa for a while?'

The smile that came easily to his lips was very natural. 'Since she started practising.' His phone rang and he snatched it up. He closed his eyes and breathed deeply, obviously listening to whoever was on the other end of the phone. 'Thanks. I appreciate it.' He hung up and looked at Claire. 'Definitely bacterial meningitis. Ring Mt Black Hospital and let them know. Hopefully, it hasn't spread to the livestock. I doubt it but make sure they're checked. Anyone who Dwight's come into contact with will need prophylactic antibiotics so get Frankie to organise that list of people. Also, if you could speak to Phyllis and see if she can remember what happened in the last few days, that would be great.'

'OK.'

Declan walked to his door. 'Let's go get this man better.' As they walked down the corridor, Claire was conscious of the looks Declan received from the female members of staff. Any of them would follow him to the ends of the earth, should he ask them. Would she? At this point in time she didn't know and that alone surprised her. She had her life all organised and she liked being in control.

'Do you want to be in Theatre?' Declan asked as they walked along.

'Can I?'

'Sure. I can arrange that.'

'Thanks. I'd appreciate it.'

'I think Phyllis would also appreciate you being in there. Someone she knows with her husband. That sort of thing. It's very comforting.'

'Yes.' Claire smiled up at him.

'What?'

'You're a very caring man, Declan.'

'I'm a doctor.'

'It's more than that and you know it.' They'd reached the isolation room and both donned masks.

'I could say the same about you.'

'What? That I'm a caring man?' Claire couldn't resist teasing as they entered and headed to the sink to wash their hands.

Declan smiled and then did something that surprised her. He leant over and placed a kiss on the tip of her nose. 'You dolt,' he said, and grinned at her. Claire was too stunned at this open display of affection to say anything.

Things moved fast then. Dwight's medication was changed to help him fight infection and Declan performed the surgery. Claire stood to the side, out of the way but still able to see. She would have enjoyed assisting him but knew she couldn't operate in the hospital for legal reasons. That thought took her mind to Dr Bean. She kicked herself for not following up with Dwight herself, but how could she have known? She'd done her job, she'd referred the patient on and had received no further communication on the subject. Declan had dictated letters to her, informing her of the treatment for each patient he'd seen. Even though she'd been in the room for half of them, he was a man who liked his i's dotted and his t's crossed, and with the impending legal action surrounding Dr Bean it was probably a good thing Declan was so fastidious.

Claire was glad when the surgery was over and she accompanied Dwight back to the isolation room, where he'd be monitored, rather than the general recovery area. Phyllis was pleased to get her husband back and sat by his bed, holding his hand.

'He'll be all right.' Declan placed his hand on Claire's shoulder as she stood by the door, looking over at her patient lying in bed. 'I can't guarantee he'll retain any hearing in his right ear but he'll live.'

'You were right, Declan. He has every right to sue the hospital, thanks to Dr Bean's negligence.'

'I'll be making an official complaint to the ENT Specialists Board of Management. This can't go unreported, Claire.'

'I understand.'

'I'm all done here and it's time to get back to Mt Black.'

'Already? You don't need to check on him later?'

'I have an appointment in Mt Black I need to keep and excellent colleagues here who will take perfect care of Dwight, and Phyllis, too.'

She'd forgotten about his appointment, the reason he couldn't make it for dinner until 7:00 p.m. She wondered if he was going to tell her what was going on.

'Do Phyllis and Dwight have any family here?'

'Yes. They're on their way,' Claire replied.

'Good. OK. Let's say goodbye and get this show on the road.'

'We get another chopper ride back?'

'Sure do,' Declan answered.

They both went over and Claire told Phyllis she was to call them any time if she was at all concerned with Dwight's condition. 'And make sure you get some rest,' she warned. 'You've had a physical shake-up with the accident this morning, not to mention all of this.'

Phyllis nodded tiredly. Declan also had a word with the nursing staff to let them know the events of that morning and for them to keep a close eye on Phyllis as well as her husband.

Claire watched as the nurses all smiled and flirted with Declan and she wasn't at all impressed. This was his other life. The one she would never be a part of. She wasn't sure whether she was glad to see it or not. For three weeks every month he'd be here, working in the hospital with all the cute nurses and female doctors fluttering their eyelashes at him. While she'd be in Mt Black, trying desperately not to think about him.

During the short flight to Mt Black, she was quiet, and when they arrived at the hospital, Claire headed directly to the clinic. She still had about an hour left of her clinic and if she could get through some patients, it would make life easier tomorrow—when everyone who'd been turned away today returned.

'Claire,' Declan called, wondering why she'd been so quiet. He quickened his pace to try and catch up with her, and succeeded as she entered the clinic building—only to find it empty, except for Bethany.

'Where are all my patients?'

'Gone.' Bethany said.

'Oh, well, that's just great.' Her words were filled with exhaustion and annoyance. 'I suppose I'm double if not triple booked for tomorrow, then.'

'No. Poncho came in and saw most of your patients. I've arranged for Declan to use the clinic rooms on Thursday afternoon after his morning operating list to catch up on his outstanding patients but basically everyone's good. Oh, and, Declan, that audiologist you organised—Louisa?'

'That's right.'

'She called through and confirmed she'd be here for a clinic on Friday.'

'Excellent. So we're free?' Declan asked.

'As a bird.' Bethany laughed. 'Unless some emergency comes in.'

'I'll pretend I didn't hear you,' he said with a smile, before turning to Claire. 'How about a relaxing cup of tea or coffee?'

Claire shook her head. 'No, thanks. I want to make a start on the files.'

'I've gone through the records,' Bethany said, 'and pulled everyone who's seen Dr Bean.'

'Thanks.' Claire nodded, sighing as she saw the huge pile stacked against the wall. 'Go home, Beth. Tomorrow's bound to be busy.'

Bethany gathered her things. 'And on Thursday I even get to be in Theatre with Declan.'

'Ooh. Party time in the OR,' Declan joked, and Bethany chuckled.

'All right. See you both tomorrow for hopefully a quieter day.'

Claire waited until Bethany had gone before watching Declan. He pulled out a chair and sat down, picking up a file. 'You're not leaving?' She couldn't meet his gaze. She knew it was childish to be jealous of his life in Brisbane but she couldn't help it. She followed suit and picked up a file, determined to just sit there and work. She had no right to quiz Declan on his life or the women who seemed to drool all over him.

'Not yet.'

'What about your appointment?'

'Appointment?'

'You mentioned you had something on this afternoon.'

'Oh, that. I don't need to go until just before four. That's one hour away and I'm hoping we can make a serious dent in these files during that time.'

'Fine.' She turned her attention to her work. She read the words written on the page but none of them sank in. She was far too aware of him as he came to sit beside her. He was watching her intently and she felt as though he'd put her beneath a microscope and was examining her closely. Not a nice feeling at all and it was difficult to control the urge to squirm.

'Claire?'

'Yes?' She didn't look up.

'What's wrong?'

'Nothing.'

'Now, see. That doesn't work. I can tell you're lying.'

'Then deal with it.'

'I'm trying to. Will you please just look at me?'

With an impatient sigh she closed the file and looked at him, a bored expression on her face.

His lips twitched. 'There. Wasn't so hard, was it?'

'What do you want, Declan?'

'For you to talk to me. Something's obviously bothering you.'

'I'm tired.'

'I know, but that's not it. Something happened in Brisbane and now you have a bee in your bonnet.'

'Where on earth does that saying come from?'

He raised his eyebrows. 'Have you ever seen someone with a bee in their hat? They flap around, all frantic like, and try not to get stung.' He waved his hands around as though there were an imaginary bee. Claire tried to stop her lips from twitching with repressed laughter and instead grabbed hold of her annoyance. 'See.' He grinned at her. 'Now, stop trying to change the subject and answer my question.'

'What?' She spread her hands wide and shrugged before crossing her arms.

'Please?' He watched her face, read her body language and noted that she was completely uncomfortable. Good. He liked it when she was off kilter. She lived her life by such rigid control and it wasn't right. He chuckled to himself. Here he was, a man who liked everything in its place, telling someone wound even tighter than he was that they needed to relax. He couldn't help it. She looked incredible when she relaxed, when she threw her arms around him and kissed him with such amazing passion. He wondered if she'd kept it bottled up for far too long. Not that he was complaining. He waited patiently but also maintained eye contact.

Claire realised he wasn't going to let it go and sighed. 'It's just… You were…different in Brisbane.'

'I was?' He was surprised at that. 'How do you mean?'

She opened her mouth to say something but closed it and shook her head. 'Look, it doesn't matter.'

'I think it does.' He waited.

'You just seemed to fit in there. Everyone admires you. You seem to have a lot of…friends.' She was referring to the number of women who'd drooled over him but Declan just shook his head, not picking up on her double meaning.

'Actually, I don't. I've only been there for six months and a lot of the other specialists are sceptical of my expertise due to my age, some are intimidated by my IQ.'

'Your peers feel threatened.' Claire stated.

'People often feel threatened by situations they don't understand. But I'm guessing that's not what's really bothering you.'

'The nursing staff don't seem to have a problem with your age or anything else about you, for that matter.'

'The nursing staff scare me silly. Well, the female nurses at any rate.'

'They do?'

'Sure. It's like being let loose in a piranha pool.'

Claire chuckled. 'That's not a nice thing to say.'

'You're right. It's not, but nevertheless that's how I feel. Again, I know I just need to settle in and then hopefully they'll realise their attempts at flirting don't work on me. I'm just uncomfortable with the attention.'

'You're a novelty.'

'Gee, thanks.'

Claire laughed again, feeling the weight lift from her heart. 'You're welcome.'

'That's what was bothering you? The nurses flirting with me?' His tone was soft.

Her smile immediately disappeared and once more she had trouble meeting his gaze.

'You don't need to be jealous, Claire.'

She lifted her chin with defiance at that comment and looked him squarely in the eyes. 'I wasn't jealous, Declan.'

His grin was a self-satisfied one. 'Oh, no? I would have been had the positions been reversed.'

'No, you wouldn't.'

'Don't bet on it.'

'But you hardly know me.'

'I beginning to realise I know a lot more about you than I initially thought. I think that also works the other way, too. You know more about me than a lot of other people.'

'Sure.' Her tone was disbelieving.

'It's true. I don't usually confess my anxiety to every person I meet, especially when I've just started a new job. Some employers might see it as a liability.'

'Compared to Dr Bean, I'll take the anxiety, thanks.'

Declan smiled and took her hand in his. 'So are we good?' Her answer was vitally important to him. This woman, who had the ability to calm him down, to give him strength. Oh, yes, she was one he wanted to hold on to and he was astounded he could feel this way after knowing her for such a short period of time.

Claire looked down at their linked hands, revelling in the warmth and tenderness of his touch. Slowly, she raised her gaze back to his. 'We're better than good.' She licked her dry lips and swallowed, noting how his gaze followed the action eagerly.

'You're flirting with me again.'

'I thought that was acceptable.'

A small smile touched his lips. 'Well…um…' he drawled, and raised one eyebrow at a rakish angle.

Claire chuckled but leaned closer to him, happy they'd cleared the air.

'Hey, sis.'

Claire jerked back and sprang up from her chair at the sound of Brett's voice. He was walking through the clinic door towards them. Immediately, she switched into concern mode. Declan drew in a breath, bracing himself for what was about to happen. With Brett here, that meant the teenager had made a decision and he knew Claire wasn't going to like it…well, not at first.

'Brett, are you all right? Upset? Did something go wrong in the exam?'

Brett shrugged and dumped his schoolbag at the base of the desk. 'I'm fine. The exam was fine.' He grinned at Declan. 'I even spoke to…some people after the exam and they did good, too.'

Declan nodded, catching the meaning of Brett's words.

'Then what are you doing here?' Claire glanced guiltily at Declan, knowing that had Brett been a fraction of a second later he would have found his big sister in a lip-lock with her new colleague.

'Meeting Declan.'

Declan saw the look of shock cross Claire's face and realised he'd just slipped a few notches on Claire's trust meter. 'You're a little early,' he said.

'Yeah. The teacher let us off early.'

'OK. Well let me finish up here and we'll get going.'

'And *where* might that be?' Claire asked, glaring at both of them in turn.

'Declan's taking me out to the golf course.' Brett grinned and rubbed his hands together. 'I get to play my first round of golf.'

Claire turned all her attention to Declan and he could tell she wasn't at all pleased. 'And when was I going to be told about these plans?'

Brett quickly jumped in. 'Don't blame Declan. I asked him not to say anything.'

Claire looked back to her brother. 'Why not?'

'I didn't think you'd let me go. This is mock exam week after all, and I know how much it means to you and the others that I study and do well. But I just…well, I just need to do something…new, and last night, Dec was telling me how he plays golf to unwind and then I asked him to take me and it just sort of went from there. But don't blame Dec. It was me. I…didn't want you to know.'

Claire was stunned. In the past Brett had often been in cahoots with either the twins or usually Thomas, but this time she was surprised it was with a non-family member. It made the lack of trust Brett had with her more painful. Why couldn't he tell her these things? She knew the answer but didn't want to acknowledge it.

Declan watched the emotions flit across Claire's face and knew he had to do something. He pulled the car keys from his pocket and tossed them to Brett, who caught them easily. 'Here you go. Put your schoolbag in the car. I'll be out in a minute.'

Brett nodded, glad to be out of the range of his sister's wrath.

'Were you going to tell me?' Claire asked the instant her brother had left.

'I promised Brett I wouldn't. I'm sorry, Claire. It was important to show him he could trust me.'

'And he can't trust me? That's what this is about, isn't it?'

'No. Not like that at all. Claire, you're like his mother.'

'And you're like the big brother. Just like you are with your own siblings.'

'But that *is* what I am. I haven't had all the responsibility thrust on me that you have. My family life and yours are two completely different situations.'

'And you don't see me interfering in yours, do you?'

'I'm not interfering.'

'I beg to differ.'

'Claire, Brett's not coping. Not coping with his workload, not coping with the pressure he feels from his teachers, from his siblings. Then there's girls in the equation.' Declan raked his hand through his hair. 'It's not an easy time for him and when you add up his stress, it makes for a volatile situation.'

'And you'd know this, how?'

'Because I've been there.' His words were forceful. 'From what I saw of Brett yesterday, he's at the stage where if he's not taught how to manage his anxiety, he'll tip over the edge into teenage depression. Trust me, Claire, you do not want that.'

'Depression? He's a happy kid.'

'No, Claire.' It hurt him to say it. 'He's not. He may portray that image to you but he's not happy.'

Claire sat down with a bump, tears glistening in her eyes. Declan knelt and took her hands in his, holding onto them when she tried to pull away.

'Look at me, Claire.'

'Go away.'

'Claire, it's not your fault Brett is the way he is. You can help him. You can give him the tools he needs to get through this. I can help you but you can't just ignore what's going on.' He paused. 'Think back over the last few months. Haven't you noticed a change in Brett?'

Claire did as he'd asked and shook her head. 'But it was just school. We all went through it. The pressure in the last year of school is enormous.'

'Yes, and it's even worse for kids with anxiety. If I hadn't had my parents there, giving me what I needed to cope, I'd have tipped over into that downward spiral. I learnt from when I was younger than Brett how to cope with my anxiety and I still struggled through that final year of school.'

'And girls? You said something about girls.'

Declan exhaled and shook his head. 'You'll need to let Brett talk to you about that when he's ready.'

'But he's already talked to you, right?'

'Claire. It's not a competition. I'm an outsider who knows *exactly* how he's feeling. I can help him and so can you.'

'He doesn't want to talk to me. Even the last few times when he's been down to the barn, I've sensed there were other things he wanted to talk about but for some reason he held off. I didn't want to push him.'

'And perhaps it was good that you didn't. It might have alienated him more.' Declan reached out and tenderly brushed away the tear that fell from her lashes and trailed down her cheek. 'It's not your fault. None of this is your fault. Know that. Believe that. You'll get him through this. He's almost a man and he needs to learn how to handle this on his own, but he'll need support from you, from all his family. A lot of the time with anxiety, it's hereditary and people express it in different ways. Chances are one of your parents had it but they were able to manage it effectively.'

'I've stuffed up again.' Claire turned away, snatching her hands from his and burying her face in them. 'I'm supposed to be his sister, not his mother.'

'You're doing a great job.'

'Obviously I'm not.' She reached for a tissue and blew her nose.

'Claire—'

'No. He's waiting. Just go, Declan. Go and talk to him and help him unwind and do whatever it is you have to do.'

Declan swallowed, seeing the pain in her eyes. She was hurting and he desperately wanted to take that hurt away, to let her know this wasn't her fault. He could say the words over and over again but he doubted they'd penetrate her set way of thinking.

'Claire, please. Don't—'

'Declan.' She glared at him. 'Just go.'

His gut twisted at the pain and confusion she was feeling and he hoped he'd be able to talk to her more later. He had to make her understand. He just had to because Claire and her family were becoming far too important to him far too quickly, and that in itself caused him more anxiety than anything else.

CHAPTER SEVEN

WHEN THE KNOCK came on the barn door, Claire ignored it, absorbed by the painting in front of her. If it was Declan, she didn't want to see him, let alone speak to him. Perhaps it was Brett? Well, she was cross with him, too. She felt as though her brother had betrayed her by confiding in Declan. She knew it was stupid but she couldn't help it. If Brett was having trouble coping with things, why hadn't he talked to her about them? She'd always been there for him. Surely he trusted her?

'Claire?'

It was Mary. Sighing, Claire put her brush down and walked to the door. She opened it and went straight back to her easel, not saying a word to her sister. Regarding the painting before her, she decided the brown wasn't exactly the right shade and mixed some more paint on her palette.

'I guess that means I can come in.' Mary paused but Claire didn't respond. 'Or I could go away if you prefer.'

Still no answer.

'Or I could just come in and talk to you and drive you so insane with my inane chatter that you'll stop shutting yourself off and talk to me.' Mary came in, closing the door behind her. She crossed to stand behind Claire and looked thoughtfully at what her sister was painting.

'Well, if a picture doesn't paint a thousand words, I don't know what does.'

'Meaning?' Claire regarded her picture critically. It was something she'd been working on for a few weeks. A man and a woman sat at a table at an outdoor café, the woman looking away, the man imploring.

'That guy looks just like Declan.'

Claire's eyes widened in horror and she stepped back, bumping into Mary, to get a better look at her artwork. 'No, he doesn't.' But even as she spoke, she realised the product of her subconscious at work.

'Oh, give it up, Claire. You're obviously hung up on the guy.'

'How can I possibly be hung up on him when I hardly know him?'

'It is possible. Believe me. That's how I felt with Greg. He came into my life in such a rush and I've never regretted getting swept up in the wave of passion and desire.'

'That was you. You were always the impulsive one.'

Mary shrugged. 'So what's the deal with Declan?'

Claire put her brush down and sighed. 'I don't know.'

'Has he kissed you?'

Claire couldn't meet her sister's gaze and instead shuffled around, capping tubes of paint and cleaning her brushes.

Mary chuckled. 'I'll take that as a yes. So what's the problem? You didn't like it?'

Claire put her brushes down and finally turned to look at her sister, despair on her face. 'I don't know, Mary.'

'Either you did or you didn't, hon.'

'Of course I did and I want him to kiss me again, but the man makes me so mad. Do you know he's taken Brett out for a game of golf?'

'Elizabeth told me.'

'What?' She was stunned and hurt. 'Did everyone know except me?'

Mary frowned. 'I'm not sure what's wrong. Why shouldn't Declan take Brett out? I think it's nice of him to take an interest in our family.'

'Yeah. Too much of an interest,' Claire mumbled.

'What's that supposed to mean?'

'Is he trying to win me over by being nice to the rest of you?

Isn't that a form of manipulation? Or is it just that he prefers spending time with my siblings rather than with me?'

Mary chuckled. 'Oh, you do have it bad. It's neither.'

'You think I'm overreacting, Mary, but I'm not. He's just waltzed into our lives and made himself at home, helping himself to our problems and trying to solve them.'

'Wait a second. What problems?'

'Did you know Brett has anxiety?'

Mary thought for a moment. 'That would explain a lot. I remember Mum getting anxious a lot. Brett's a lot like her in personality.'

Claire frowned. 'I don't remember that.'

'That's because you were always second in charge. When things became too much for Mum, you took over. You helped with the twins, with Thomas and Brett. You just pitched in, did what you were supposed to do, and in some ways it took away your right to be a normal child, Claire.'

The words echoed her conversation with Declan last night. 'But you noticed Mum's anxiety?'

'I guess as I wasn't the oldest, the pressure wasn't so great.'

'But you always helped, too.'

'Not in the ways you did.' Mary sat down in the chair and indicated Claire should do the same. 'You're wonderful at being in charge and none of us would have got through those really hard times without you and your strength, but it's time for you to rest, big sister.'

'I can't rest. Brett still has his final exams. He has no idea what he wants to do when he finishes school and now to be told by a man I hardly know that my brother has anxiety makes me feel—' Claire broke off as she slumped down into the chair.

'Makes you feel as though you've failed Brett.'

'Yes.'

'Oh, Claire.' Mary went and sat on the arm of Claire's chair and comforted her. 'You're nuts. You haven't failed any of us. I doubt if you ever could. I'm sure Brett doesn't even understand his feelings and sometimes it takes someone from the outside, coming in with a completely fresh view, to realise what's been there all along. Surely you do that with patients in your clinics?'

'I guess.' Claire paused. 'He said if Brett didn't learn how to control the anxiety, he'd start on a downward spiral.'

'Teenage depression?' Mary raised her eyebrows.

'Yes. I've seen cases of it in the past and the longer it goes unchecked, the harder it can be to help the person.'

'Then shouldn't we be thankful Declan is here? I presume he's dealt with these things before and, being a man and an outsider, it may be better for Brett to get help from him rather than one of us.'

'But we're his family.'

'That's right. Perhaps he felt if he told us how he was feeling, he'd feel as though he'd let us down. He knows how much we've all sacrificed, you in particular. None of us want you to be disappointed in us. We all want to succeed and probably Brett most of all. Not only does he have you but the rest of us as well. We've all been responsible for raising him and he might think if he fails any of his subjects he would have let us all down in one fell swoop.'

Claire looked at Mary. 'When did you get so smart?'

Mary laughed, not taking offence. 'Being married has changed me. I see things differently, and besides, not being around day in, day out does have its advantages.'

'Gives you perspective.'

'Yes.'

'Did we put too much pressure on Brett?'

Mary shrugged. 'Never intentionally.'

'I feel so…flawed.'

Both women were silent for a few minutes. 'What are you going to do about Declan?'

Claire sighed. 'I have no idea.'

'Why don't you just try dating him?'

'I don't date.'

'Is that because of Ken?'

There was a knock at the door and then Declan's voice called, 'Claire? Is it OK if I come in?'

Mary headed for the door.

'No.' Claire whispered, trying to snag her sister's arm. 'Don't go.'

'You need to talk,' Mary whispered back, before flinging open the door.

'Mary.' Declan looked from one sister to the other. 'Sorry if I'm interrupting. I can talk to Claire later.' Even though he said the words, he didn't move.

'It's fine, Declan. I'll go up and check on dinner. See you both in about ten minutes.'

'Thanks,' Declan said, and as Mary walked past him, she winked.

'Good luck,' she whispered.

He tried not to smile and realised that where Mary was concerned, he had an ally. She was close to her sister and probably a confidante, and by the faint pink tinge to Claire's cheeks, he could easily guess what they'd just been discussing. He still stood outside the door. 'Is it all right if I come in?'

'Guess so.' She returned to the task of cleaning her brushes and was so focused on trying to ignore him that she forgot about his likeness in the painting until it was too late.

'Nice painting,' Declan said, and then stopped to peer more closely at it. 'That woman looks very much like you.'

Claire closed her eyes and waited for the next set of words.

'What did I do wrong?'

She opened her eyes and turned to find him not looking at the painting but at her. 'You know perfectly well what you did wrong.'

'Not with Brett.' He indicated the painting. 'In there. By the look on your face, I've done something terribly wrong.' He returned to studying it. 'You really are exceptionally clever.'

She set her brushes to soak and packed away the last of her paints before removing her painting shirt and scrubbing her hands. She wasn't sure what to make of him, either here in person or in the painting. 'How's Brett?'

Declan shrugged. 'He's studying.'

'Good.' Again, she found it difficult to look at him. 'Golf game was fun?'

'Yes. He said he hadn't played before. The kid's a natural.'

'Great,' she muttered. 'The boy has an intelligent mind and will probably end up being a professional golfer.'

'Hey. I'll have you know golf isn't just about hitting a little white ball about on fuzzy green grass. It's—'

'Leave it,' Claire said. 'I was being ironic.'

'Oh.' He shut his mouth for a moment. 'So is this a good time for me to grovel and beg for forgiveness?'

'No.'

'Will any time be a good time or are you just shutting me out?'

Claire flicked off the taps, dried her hands and turned to face him. 'Look, Declan, you've been honest with me so it's only fair I offer you the same courtesy. I know we're attracted to each other but it isn't going to work.'

'What isn't?'

'This. This thing between us.' She indicated the space between them.

'And what is this "thing"?'

'You know.'

'Obviously I don't, otherwise I wouldn't need you to spell it out for me.'

'This flirting we keep doing,' she said huffily.

'We do?'

'Declan. Cut it out.'

He shook his head. 'Claire, what's wrong with getting to know each other? I'll admit I might have rushed in like a bull in a china shop where the attraction between us is concerned, but I've also been weighing up lots of pros and cons with regard to anything permanent between us.'

'See. You've thought about it.'

'And you haven't?' he asked, his tone sceptical. 'You can't tell me you haven't or we wouldn't be having this conversation.' Part of her wanted him to bridge the gap between them, to take her in his arms and kiss her because that was the only time she felt as though her world was back on an even keel. 'Sometimes, when people meet each other and the attraction is there, things move fast. It's just the way things happen. That's the way it's happening in this case. I'll be gone on Saturday morning and I want to use the remaining time until then to get to know you better. That's what I'm asking. I'm not talking about marriage, or having children or any of those other permanent relationship things that you're so concerned about.'

Claire couldn't understand why she felt a sense of forlornness at his words but immediately strengthened her resolve. She *didn't* want any relationships. She *didn't* want a permanent man in her life. That wasn't the future she'd planned.

'Well…good, because I've done my time. I've raised my siblings, I've made sure they were safe and healthy. I've taken over doing the bills, balanced the cheque books, found the money to pay for Mary's wedding. I've done all that and I'm not going to do it again. I deserve some peace and solitude. I deserve to be able to do my own thing.'

'I'm not disputing that. I don't want to take you away from your family, I don't want to compete for your attention. I like your siblings, Claire. They're a credit to you.' He took a step closer. 'But I like you—as a person, as a woman. Yes, I'm interested in you and I can't say for certain where things may end up, but right now getting to know you, spending time with you is what I'd like to do. I'd also like to say, for the record, that you would make a fantastic mother to your own children…should you decide one day to have some.'

She laughed without humour. 'Like the way I've raised Brett?'

'There's nothing wrong with Brett. It's the anxiety. Everyone gets anxious at some point, like when they're afraid. It's a general response that is out of proportion to environmental threats. There are also different types of anxiety but there are also programmes being taught through schools that help children deal with it.'

'What type does Brett have?'

'At this stage, I'd say general anxiety, which is worrying about his future as well as his past. He has a social phobia but that's more his age than anything else.'

'What's that?'

'Being humiliated, embarrassed in public.'

Claire rolled her eyes. 'Even I have that.'

Declan smiled. 'A lot of people do but with Brett the feelings are intensified, especially where girls are concerned.'

'Does he have a girlfriend?'

'No, but, like any normal teenage boy, he likes someone.'

'See. There it is again. He's talking to you and not to me.'

'It's not your fault, Claire. Be glad he's talking. You've taught him how to trust and now he's making the decision about who to trust with what. I wouldn't be surprised if each one of your siblings knows a bit—just a small bit—about what's going on in Brett's life. If you all sat down together and openly discussed it, you'd get a much clearer picture. Regardless of that, be glad he's actually talking. It's vitally important for kids his age to talk.'

'What about kids your age?'

'What do you think I'm doing now?' He smiled at her. 'I psychoanalyse, I churn things over, I don't sleep.' He shrugged. 'I'm used to it but if I don't talk things out, it gets worse.'

'Hence your honesty.'

'Yes.'

'What types of anxiety do you have?'

'Now? General. I worry about the past and future. I have the odd panic attack—you know, palpitations, chest pain, difficulty breathing, that sort of thing—but they're not that often and I'm getting better with my social phobia.'

'You sound so calm about it all.'

'Because I've accepted it. It's the same as any other long-term health problem. Acceptance goes a long way to effective management. I used to have separation anxiety and depression so I'm quite happy with where I am now. I can see how I've grown, changed, and it's all for the better.'

'And this is what I need to teach Brett?'

'What we all need to help Brett with. I can put you in touch with someone who runs an anxiety programme for teenagers, although it may be best for him to start that once his school year is over.'

'And in the meantime?'

'I can teach you the basics to get him through the next few months.'

Claire sighed. 'I don't know if I can, Declan. I mean, he doesn't trust me.'

Declan shook his head. 'You're wrong. He trusts you, Claire, but he trusts you as a mother figure. He looks up to you, he takes his cues from you. He's trying to be like you, can't you see that? He's trying to be in control, to do what's expected of him, to not let anyone down.'

'I've never put that type of pressure on him.'

'No, but he's put it on himself. You're a shining example of what he wants to become, perhaps what he feels he *must* become.'

'And that adds more pressure?'

'Yes.'

Tears glazed her eyes and she choked back a sob. 'When did I stop being his sister? Why can't I just be his sister? Why did I have to be his mother? It's not fair, Declan.'

He was beside her in an instant and when he pulled her into his arms, she went willingly, glad of the comfort he was offering. He held her, kissing her head every now and then as she cried. His heart filled with compassion for her and her situation. Once more the protective urge asserted itself and he knew without a doubt that whatever happened between himself and Claire, he needed to help her and her family through this. It was as though he'd come to Mt Black specifically for that reason but he hadn't known it until now.

When she started to settle, she pulled back, feeling embarrassed. 'What was it you said about social phobias?' She took a tissue and blew her nose, smiling at him, knowing her nose would be red and her eyes swollen.

'Don't be embarrassed, Claire.'

'Look at me, Declan.'

'I am.' His words were simple and matter-of-fact and made her feel more comforted than ever before. 'I see you, Claire. All of you. What you were, what you've become. And I like it.'

'So we're back to discussing us?'

'All roads lead to Rome.'

She walked to the sink and had a quick drink of water before turning to face him. 'So what now?'

'Now? I'd like to spend some time with you. That doesn't mean I want to take you away from what you usually do but perhaps we could have dinner. Alone? Just the two of us. At a restaurant?'

'As in a date?'

'Exactly. Don't you think the attraction we feel is worth exploring?'

'Are you going to over-think it? Analyse it?'

He laughed humourlessly. 'Without a doubt. Once the process begins, it's actually hard to stop.'

Claire nodded. 'Do we flaunt this…non-relationship?'

'I'll let you decide on that. It's your home, your hospital, your town. You need to be comfortable with things because I'll be gone at the end of the week.'

Again, when he said the words she felt a sense of panic, of possessiveness. She wanted to hold him and tell him not to leave her. That although it had been such a short time since he'd exploded into her life, she wasn't sure she would be the same without him. It was ridiculous but nevertheless that was exactly the way she felt.

'I'm not sure.'

'Then we can play it by ear. I'll let you set the pace.'

'Meaning?'

'If you want to hold my hand in public, you may.'

'Gee, thanks.'

He smiled. 'If you want to grab me and kiss me, feel free.'

She tried not to be amused but found she was fighting a losing battle. 'How generous of you.'

'I'm a generous kind of guy,' he said with a shrug. 'Like now. I'm letting you stay on that side of the room. See? You're calling the shots.'

Claire shrugged. 'I don't have to call *all* of them.'

'Meaning?'

'Meaning get over here and kiss me.'

Declan's smile broadened. 'Why, Dr Neilson, I thought you'd never ask.' Even with his words, he didn't rush but slowly made his way across. Once he was standing in front of her, he reached out a hand and tenderly brushed her hair from her eyes. 'I'm sorry I hurt you,' he murmured, meeting her gaze.

'Will you shut up and kiss me?'

'If you insist.' Declan did as he was told and Claire sighed into his embrace. This was where she'd wanted to be ever since that morning when he'd pressed his mouth against hers with such passion. Every time they came together, the feelings became more intense and now was no exception. He was right, so very right to say this natural chemistry that existed between them was worth exploring. He'd also said he didn't usually act on impulse and neither did she, but this was one time when both seemed content to throw caution to the wind and see where they ended up.

'Claire,' he murmured against her mouth.

'Shh.' She deepened the kiss, wanting to forget all the questions she had. She knew she was acting out of character but right now it felt so wonderful, so free to be impulsive. At the same time, she worked hard to suppress the growing emotions he evoked in her. All she wanted was to be swept away, floating on a cloud, feeling light-headed and loving it.

'Claire.' Once more, the sound of her name on Declan's lips brought her back to reality, but this time he'd said it more as in a dream, one she realised they'd both been captured in. Did he want to lose himself in her, just as she did in him? It was something to ponder…later…much later.

He broke his mouth from hers, both of them gasping for air. Soft kisses were pressed to her neck as he nuzzled with increasing hunger. 'This will get out of hand if we let it.' His words were barely audible.

'We won't,' she whispered.

Declan pulled back and looked down at her face. Her eyes were closed, the worry lines she perpetually wore had disappeared and she looked relaxed and happy. His male pride increased, realising he was the one who'd made her feel this way. 'Although I don't want to say this…'

Claire opened her eyes and placed two fingers across his lips. 'Then don't.'

He smiled and kissed her fingertips. 'Your family is waiting.'

She sighed heavily and shifted from his embrace. 'You're right. I hate it but you're right.'

Declan considered her for a moment. 'Do you ever get away?'

Claire spread her arms wide, indicating the room. 'This is how I get away.'

'I meant go away, for a break, a holiday.'

'Holiday? What's that?'

'Never?'

'I've been to the odd conference in Brisbane but the last one was two years ago.' She fussed around the room, finishing her cleaning and packing away. 'With Brett doing his final years of school, we've all stayed close. Jason was overseas earlier in the year to attend a cooking course, Thomas has been to Brisbane a few times for special seminars for uni—that sort of thing. But that's about it. So it's not only me who's making sacrifices.'

'You need a break.'

'You're preaching to the choir.' She shut off the light and as they stepped out into the darkness, Declan automatically slipped his hand into hers and she didn't protest in the slightest.

They were silent for a minute before Claire spoke. 'You said Brett would get anxious over girls. Do you?'

'Yes.'

She raised her eyebrows, surprised. 'Really?' An inquisitive feminine smile came onto her lips. 'About me?'

'I've already told you I didn't sleep much last night.'

'Because of me?' Her smile was now quite smug. She'd had no idea she affected him so much.

Declan chuckled. 'You have no idea how twisted into knots I am. I've known you for such a short time. It's ridiculous.'

'But it feels so right.'

'Exactly.'

Claire nodded and squeezed his hand before letting go. 'Well, you're not the only one who's anxious about it.' She opened the door.

'Glad I'm not out on that ledge all by myself,' he said softly as they entered the big house.

Once more Jason outdid himself with dinner, especially the delicious crème brûlée for dessert. 'You're spoiling me, Jason.

When I return to Brisbane, I have to contend with omelettes or TV dinners.'

'Yuck. That's disgusting, Dec,' Jason muttered. 'I'll write down some restaurants in Brisbane where you can get a good meal.'

'I'm guessing the hospital cafeteria won't be on that list.'

Jason gave him a scornful look. 'Absolutely not.'

Declan laughed and helped clear the plates.

'You'll have to make sure you come over for at least a few meals every time you're in town,' Mary said pointedly, giving her sister little glances. Claire ignored her.

'Declan,' Brett said. 'Got a bit of time to help me with my maths?'

'Sure.' Once more he settled at the table with Brett and went over a few things. Claire watched while she stacked the dishwasher, marvelling at how selflessly the man seemed to give of himself. When he was done, both of them reviewed Elizabeth's arm. Satisfied with her progress, he announced it was time for him to leave.

'I don't want you to think I'm forcing you to go,' Claire said as she walked him to the car.

'You're not. I have a phone call to make and I don't want to leave it too late.'

'Oh.' Claire lowered her gaze to the ground, wanting to ask but not wanting to pry.

'It's just to my dad,' he volunteered.

'You're very close to your parents,' she commented.

'Yes. I guess it's not common for a man of my age to keep in such close contact with his parents, but I don't care. They're both good friends of mine and I think it's quite sad the number of people who, once they leave home, seem to forget or want to escape their upbringing.'

Claire nodded. 'I think it's wonderful you're close.'

Declan detected the wistfulness in her voice and gathered her to him. 'Sorry. I didn't mean to say anything that might—'

'It's all right.' She rested her head against his chest. 'Some days I miss them more than others.'

He placed a kiss on the top of her head and held her, knowing instinctively that was all she needed from him at that moment. Finally, she pulled back.

'I'll see you tomorrow.'

'Yes.'

'Will you sleep tonight?'

'Maybe.'

'Even if I do this?' She stood on tiptoe and pressed her lips to his.

'That might help me sleep.'

'What about this?' She kissed him once more, adding a hint of lascivious tongue.

Declan growled and deepened the kiss, hauling her close against his body. 'No,' he said after a few hungry moments, his breathing erratic. 'That won't help at all.'

'Oh.' Her eyes were wide with mockery. 'Then I won't do that.'

'Minx.' Declan pressed one more firm kiss to her lips before putting her from him.

'Go tell your dad all about me,' she said.

'He already knows,' Declan offered as he opened the car door and climbed in. His words surprised Claire.

'Oh,' she said again, but this time her emotions were genuine. 'OK. Now I feel self-conscious.'

'No need to.' He smiled, knowing he had to change the subject and quickly, otherwise he'd be wanting to haul her against him once more. He had to drive back to the motel and he was concerned he wouldn't concentrate properly on the road, his mind and body only wanting more of the woman before him. His mind searched for the easiest switch—work. 'Do you spend much time in an operating theatre?'

'Er…none.' She was startled at his sudden change in topic.

'Would you like to?'

'Uh…sure. Why?'

'Well, I'm scheduled to do a laryngectomy on Thursday. They're not all that common and I doubt you'd have come across many in Mt Black. I thought you might like to be in Theatre.'

'Arn Jacobs.' Claire nodded and saw the big picture to Declan's words. Arn had been a good friend of her parents and a patient of hers since she'd started practising medicine here in Mt Black. He was seventy-four and alternating between depression and denial about having this surgery. Being diagnosed with throat cancer had been bad enough but being told he needed to have the cancer excised by removal of the larynx was something Arn had struggled to deal with.

Thankfully, Arn had insisted on getting a second opinion rather than taking Dr Bean's word for it. Claire had set the appointment up with an ENT specialist in Brisbane which had turned out to be Declan. It was a small world and amazing the way it revolved. That was another reason why she'd been even more eager to meet him when he'd first arrived in Mt Black. Knowing she'd be in the theatre might put Arn at ease. It would also give her a look at exactly what Declan would be doing as she would be responsible for Arn's health care once Declan left at the end of the week. 'Yes,' she said more firmly. 'I'd really like to be there. Thanks for asking.'

He shrugged. 'No problem. I have house calls tomorrow, which I think I'm doing with someone else.'

'Cathy. She's our ambulance driver. She'll take you.'

'Right, but I will see you some time tomorrow?'

Claire smiled. 'You can count on it, even if I have to drag you into a clinic room and lock the door.'

She laughed when he groaned. 'Claire!' He started the engine and reversed, the headlights illuminating her, leaving him with a vision of an angel surrounded by a halo of light. Was that what she was? His angel? The woman he'd always known would one day come into his life and change it for ever?

'So much for changing the subject,' he muttered, and wound down his window, getting hit with a blast of cold air. He needed it to help him think straight on the drive back to town because Claire Neilson had him all in an adolescent dither…but he liked it.

CHAPTER EIGHT

WEDNESDAY was exhausting. Declan hadn't done house calls like this since…well, since for ever. It wasn't part of his job, working in big city hospitals, but out here, where many people lived on properties an hour or two out of Mt Black, house calls were a must.

Cathy, the ambulance officer, was a jovial woman about the same age as his grandmother. She chatted all day long and Declan enjoyed it, knowing the occasional murmur was sufficient enough to keep her going.

'And our Claire does a wonderful job. That hospital board doesn't appreciate what she does. It would just be nice if they gave her more credit but I guess the way the locals feel about her, she gets her praise. We all think she's wonderful. Our little Claire, we call her. Done a marvellous job with raising her siblings. Pity, though. The poor girl gets no time to herself.' Cathy's eyes sparkled as she spoke.

'You should take her away, Dr Silvermark. Show her the big city. Help her let her hair down.'

Declan smiled politely, knowing Cathy was hoping for some gossip. She already knew that Declan had eaten with the Neilson family twice so he guessed they were already being talked about. 'I don't think Claire appreciates the city. The twenty-four-hour shopping and bright lights wouldn't interest her much.' He paused, glancing across at Cathy, unable to give the locals something more to talk about. 'But the art gallery might be the place to take her.'

'Whoo-hoo, yes, it would.' Cathy laughed. 'Glad to see you're watching out for her.'

Declan nodded and listened to Cathy's chatter as she headed back to town. When she dropped him at the hospital, he was surprised to find it was almost six o'clock in the evening.

'What took you so long?' Claire asked when Declan walked through to the clinic.

'You done here?'

'Yes. Bethany's just left. I was about to lock up when I saw the ambulance come in.' She smiled at him. 'Busy day?'

'You could say that. I'm exhausted.'

Claire laughed. 'I'm not surprised. All that chatter from Cathy.'

Declan rubbed his ears and smiled. 'Anyway, you ready to go?'

'No. I've just got one more patient to see.'

'Oh?' Declan looked around the deserted waiting room.

Claire walked over and ran her fingers down his tie, picking up the end and holding it firmly in her hand. 'You. Clinic room one.' She tugged at his tie. 'Now.'

Declan grinned and followed her in, liking this joyful side of her. 'Where are all your inhibitions, Claire?'

'Not sure, Declan.' She raised an eyebrow. 'Complaining?'

'Definitely not,' he said as he kicked the door shut and pulled her into his arms. It felt so good to be holding her. It was what he'd wanted all day long and now that he'd managed to somehow live through house calls, it was as though he was getting his reward.

'I missed you today,' she confessed shyly.

'I missed you, too.'

'Coming to my place for dinner?'

He smiled and brushed a kiss across her lips. 'Not tonight. I need to get through those files.'

'I can help you.'

'It's all right. You've done enough. Besides, it's not as though I'm going to sleep much.'

'Am I still affecting you, Dr Silvermark?'

'Way too much.' He bent his head and captured her lips with

his, wondering if he'd ever get enough of her. She was generous, caring, understanding, to name just a few of her attributes, and Declan realised she was the type of woman he'd been searching for. Yet all she wanted was peace and solitude. He scoffed at that idea. Claire would be bored within ten minutes. Couldn't she see that? She needed people around her. She was a giver and as such she needed to be able to give.

After a while, they locked up the clinic and he walked her to her car.

'Offer's still open.'

Declan smiled but shook his head, glancing down at his briefcase on the ground, which was now full of hospital casenotes. 'This needs doing. Go and relax. Finish painting, read a book. Have some "Claire" time.'

'I'm not sure I know what that is.'

Declan reached around and unclipped her hair from the ponytail, loving the way the blond strands cascaded down around her face. He laced his fingers through the strands, groaning at the soft, silky texture before massaging the back of her neck with his thumbs. 'You need to unwind more, Claire.'

'You help me unwind.'

'Really? That's nice.'

'I'm going to miss you when you go.'

'I'll be back in three weeks.' Even as he said the words, it seemed like a very long time. Three weeks. Three weeks of not being able to see her, to speak to her, to touch her, the way he was doing now. It was going to be like crawling through a desert. He bent and pressed a quick kiss to her lips before dropping his hands and taking two steps back. 'See you tomorrow.'

'Don't work too hard.'

'We'll have dinner together tomorrow night. Yes?'

'Yes,' she confirmed, and watched as he climbed into his car and drove away. He was keeping his distance. He wasn't getting too close and she should appreciate that. She wasn't into relationships. She had enough to deal with in her everyday life without complicating things with romantic entanglements, but, if she was going to be honest, she would acknowledge she was already romantically entangled with Declan…and she loved it.

The following morning, Declan did a pre-operative review of his patients and checked out the small operating theatre. He was standing in the doorway, looking in to the operating room when he sensed Claire's presence.

'I hope everything meets with your approval?' she said from behind him. He turned and looked at her, his gaze gently caressing her body, a hungry smile coming easily to his lips.

'Absolutely.'

She rolled her eyes and her smile increased. 'I was talking about the operating theatre.'

He raised an eyebrow. 'So was I.'

'Sleep well?'

'Sort of. And you?'

'Sort of.'

Declan watched her closely for a moment, his smile increasing. Although neither of them spoke, the silent conversation they had was extremely interesting. 'You really are good at flirting,' he said softly.

'Was I flirting?'

'Doing it unconsciously now, eh?'

Claire chuckled but didn't reply. Instead, she headed into the scrub area. 'Theatre Sister will be here soon. Have you asked if I can watch?'

'Do I need her permission?'

Claire frowned. 'Things work differently in a small hospital and, besides, Theatre Sister's husband is a member of the hospital board. They may think it an inefficient use of my time to be in Theatre.'

'Then they're going to have me to deal with.' Declan checked his watch. 'We've got half an hour before the list starts—let's go to the clinic kitchen and have a cuppa.' Claire nodded her agreement and without a word followed him out. It wasn't until they both had drinks and were sitting at the small table in the room that she spoke.

'The people on the hospital board have been here…for ever,

it seems. Now, sometimes that's a good thing but other times…'
She shook her head.

'They have trouble moving forward.'

'Yes. I'm sure most of them still look upon me as little Claire Neilson who broke her arm when she was six years old.'

'They're all ex-doctors?'

'Only two of them.'

'Then don't they realise how difficult it is for you?'

'*They* got by.'

'I'm sure the population of Mt Black was a lot less then than it is now.'

'Some days, it feels as though it's tripled.'

'Do they trust you?'

'Medically? Yes. They're more than confident in my abilities and, as they so often point out, there are other doctors in Mt Black who provide health care for the people. Which is very true.'

'But what about on-call, after-hours work?'

'Again, there is a roster and the other GPs take their turn. It's just that every time I want them to add something or review something, it's a song and dance routine.'

'Like getting phones in the clinic rooms?'

'Exactly. That won't happen for at least another year and it's not because there isn't the funding. It's just that they don't think it's necessary. The money could be used on other things.'

'But there are always other things and when you have specialists coming in once a month to hold clinics, they expect certain standards.'

'True.'

'What if *I* put in a request?'

'I doubt they'd listen. You're just here for one week per month, like the others. Usually, when things get bad, I go to Poncho.'

'He's in your corner?'

Claire nodded. 'He was the one who pushed the board to finally get rid of Dr Bean. I'd asked on at least two occasions for them to review him.'

'Let me guess, Dr Bean was a friend of someone on the board?'

'Yes.'

'Well, Dr Bean could end up costing them a tidy sum. When do you think I'll be able to speak to Ken?'

Claire shook her head. 'He's not available until next week.'

'Convenient. Is he related to someone on the board?'

'Yes, as a matter of fact he is, but that's not why. He's at a legal conference in Brisbane.'

'If he's not averse to meeting in Brisbane, he can see me there next week.'

Claire nodded. 'I'll see what I can do.'

'No. I'll contact him. You've got more than enough to do.'

She wasn't sure how she felt about that. The man she was interested in was going to contact the man she'd once been engaged to. Should that make her feel uncomfortable? It really shouldn't matter but in a small way she felt a bit paranoid. She and Ken were friends. In fact, Claire got along very well with Ken's wife. So she shouldn't have any worry about Declan talking to Ken. No. She was just being ridiculous and, besides, Declan was just a new colleague…one who made her feel immensely special and who kissed like a dream. It wasn't as though there was anything serious between them. She didn't do serious relationships.

'Claire? Claire?'

'What? Sorry.'

Declan smiled. 'You were miles away.'

'Yes.' She sipped at her tea and glanced at him. 'Are we still on for dinner tonight?'

Declan's smile increased. 'Absolutely. How was dinner last night?'

'Everyone complained because you weren't there.'

'And Brett?'

Claire sighed. 'He studied hard and seemed to have coped with his exam yesterday.'

Declan nodded.

'Whatever you said to him when you were playing golf seems to have helped.'

'Good. I'm glad.'

'I'm sorry I flew off the handle about that.'

'Don't apologise. You had every right to be annoyed.'

'Really?'

'So where shall we go tonight? Any good restaurants in town? Do I need to book somewhere?'

Claire smiled as she stood and took her cup to the sink. 'This is Mt Black, Declan. No need to book. I have house calls later today so I'll drop by your motel and collect you from there.'

'Okey-dokey.' He grinned at her and stood. As she went to walk past him, he reached for her arm and spun her into his arms. 'Let me thank you in advance for a nice evening.'

Claire placed one hand on his chest, not sure whether that was to support herself or to push him away. All she knew was he felt warm and firm beneath her touch and she liked it. Within a split second he'd lowered his head, his lips capturing hers in a heart-stopping kiss.

It was as though they'd never parted. That since last night when he'd kissed her goodnight, they'd been connected but now they were both recharging themselves.

'Well, this is an interesting new development,' a voice said from the doorway, and Claire edged back, but Declan took his time letting her go. She turned to see Bethany lounging in the doorway. Trying for composure, Claire stepped away from Declan. She looked from Bethany to Declan and back again, knowing her face was now glowing red. Opening her mouth to defend herself, she closed it just as quickly, shook her head and walked from the room.

Bethany laughed and walked into the room. 'Just getting ready for your operating list?'

Declan smiled. 'Something like that.' He picked up his cup from the table and drank the contents.

'I, for one, think it's a good development.'

'Really?'

'Yes. Claire's been shut off for too long. She needs someone in her life.'

'She has five siblings,' Declan pointed out.

Bethany nodded. 'Five siblings who aren't afraid to pursue lives of their own.'

'Thanks to Claire.'

'Yes, thanks to Claire. She's sacrificed way too much and she needs to realise it's time to stop and to focus on herself, but in a good way.' Bethany fixed him with a pointed stare. 'She doesn't need to be hurt.'

He nodded, heeding the warning before rinsing his cup. 'You're very protective of her.'

Bethany smiled. 'You'll find all the locals are.'

'Interesting. Thanks for the advice. You still joining me in Theatre?'

'A laryngectomy? I wouldn't miss it for the world.'

'Good.' Declan headed back the way he'd come and went to change before checking with the anaesthetist. 'Everything ready?'

'He's almost out,' the anaesthetist informed him.

'Excellent.' He headed to the scrub sink, looking around every now and then. There was no sign of Claire and he wondered whether she'd changed her mind or whether Theatre Sister had changed it for her. It wasn't until Mr Jacobs was anaesthetised that Declan saw Claire through the window into the scrub room where Bethany was helping her to finish gowning.

'Is there something you need, Dr Silvermark?' Theatre Sister asked icily.

Declan cleared his throat and returned his attention to the theatre. 'I've asked Dr Neilson to observe Mr Jacob's surgery. I feel that way she can provide a more detailed explanation to the patient as well as monitor him more effectively.' He looked at the sister and saw the disapproving twitch of her eyebrows. He was sure her lips were pursed tightly beneath her mask.

'Very good, Doctor.'

Claire walked into the room and Declan winked at her before glancing at the other staff members. Everyone seemed a little on edge and as he was the lead surgeon, it was up to him to keep things under control. 'I'm not sure how many of you have assisted with a laryngectomy before so I'll talk things through as I'm doing it.' He looked around the room. 'If you have any queries or questions, don't be too shy to ask.

'Today we'll be performing a total laryngectomy to remove Mr Jacob's cancer. The tumour hasn't responded to radiotherapy so this is our only course of action to save Mr Jacob's life. I'll begin with a resection of the hyoid bone, pre-epiglottic space, thyroid cartilage, cricoid cartilage and one to four trachael rings. Once we've removed the cancer, I'll suture the trachea to the skin of the neck and then we can start on the reconstruction and insertion of the artificial larynx.'

Declan made eye contact with each team member and received a nod of understanding. 'Let's get started,' he said, and held out his hand for the scalpel.

The operation was long and meticulous and he had to remember to be very specific in his instructions, but as they neared the end he was very proud of the staff here at this small hospital.

'All right. If we can get the airway tube into the trachea so Mr Jacobs can breathe, we'll be almost finished,' Declan announced.

By the time they came out of Theatre, Claire was smothering another yawn. Declan smiled as he continued to degown. 'I guess surgery takes a bit of getting used to.'

'How do you do it? Standing in one place for so long?'

He chuckled and sat down to write up the notes. 'What time do you need to leave for house calls?'

'Soon.'

'I hope I haven't made you late for them.'

'No.'

'Do you get driven around by Cathy?'

Claire smiled. 'Yes.'

'Hmm.' He nodded. 'Should be interesting for you, then.'

'Why? You've got me worried now.'

'Cathy, along with a lot of other people in Mt Black, think you work too hard and need a break. I have to say, I agreed with her.'

'And?'

'And she thought I should be the one to help you relax. She knew I'd had dinner with you.'

Claire groaned. 'They're all gossiping, aren't they?'

'Yes.' He placed a hand on her shoulder. 'You all right with that?'

She dragged in a breath and tried to calm herself down. Why

should she be upset? There was nothing really going on between herself and Declan…just a bit of an interlude. He'd be gone by the end of the week and everything would return to normal…at least until next month when he came back. Claire frowned. 'Guess I'm going to have to be. Anyway, we'll be seen together tonight so that will definitely give their tongues something to wag about. Thanks for the heads-up.'

'You're welcome. As I have a small clinic this afternoon and you're out gallivanting about, why don't we meet at the motel coffee shop? That way, if you're running late, it won't matter.'

'Sounds good.' She indicted her scrubs. 'I guess I'd better change before heading out. It might scare the patients to see me dressed like this.' She headed for the door then stopped. 'Er…thanks for letting me be there for Arn's surgery. I appreciate it.'

Declan gave her his hundred-watt smile, and Claire quickly went to the female locker room where she'd left her clothes and began to change. It wouldn't do for her to melt into a puddle of desire at his feet. In fact, she shouldn't do that now or ever.

It was high time she got a grip on reality. Declan Silvermark would be here today and gone tomorrow…well, within a few days anyway. He'd go back to his life in Brisbane, where nurses flirted with him, colleagues remained wary of him and he could play golf with his father every Saturday. Back to a life that didn't include her or her siblings. Sure, there was something between them but she'd already told him she wasn't looking for a relationship. A permanent connection was the furthest thing from her mind at the moment.

Wasn't it?

Claire paused on her way out and stared at her reflection in the mirror. She'd had to remind herself quite a bit this week that, regardless of what her rapidly growing feelings were for Declan, they meant nothing in the long run.

She shook her head and acknowledged the truth. She was more interested in him than in any other man from her past and she'd known him less than a week. This time last week her life had been on the usual path, the usual even-keeled existence, and now…now…she didn't know which way was up.

The man had her completely in knots. She'd fought against the aching need for one of his smiles and when it came, she invariably hyperventilated, rather than reacting like a normal person and simply smiling back. She'd fought the jealousy when he gave others his undivided attention, wishing he'd give more of it to her. She'd fought the need to have his arms around her and his lips pressed to hers but when she was finally in his embrace, she never wanted to be out of it.

She glared at her reflection. 'What's wrong with you?' she whispered fiercely. She had her nice, quiet life planned out. Get her siblings settled and married off and then she would be free to relax and enjoy the peace and quiet she had coming to her.

So why did that now sound so boring?

Slowly her gaze widened as she stared more closely at herself in the mirror. She covered her mouth with her hand and shook her head. 'No. Oh, no.'

The truth of the situation was there before her. Her symptoms added up to the only conclusive diagnosis: she was in love with Declan.

CHAPTER NINE

IT WAS RIDICULOUS. She shook her head, denying the truth. She couldn't possibly be in love with him. She'd only known him for what? Four days. No. It was ridiculous, that's what it was. People didn't fall in love that soon and especially with people they hardly knew anything about.

But you do know him, her heart reasoned. He's considerate, truthful and decent. He's a man who cares, who protects, who goes out of his way to help the helpless. Did that mean he saw *her* as helpless? A helpless, lovelorn woman? Was he only being nice to her and her family as a way of passing his time here in Mt Black?

No. She dismissed the notion the instant it entered her head. She knew him better than that. And in that instant she realised she did. People could spend hours, days, weeks, even years with each other and still *never* connect the way she connected with Declan. This was something very special they had going and both would be mad to ignore it.

She checked her reflection again but the evidence was still conclusive. The question was, what did she do about it?

Claire rushed through her house calls that afternoon, ignoring most of Cathy's chatter and making noncommittal replies, knowing she needed to talk to Declan when they met for dinner. When she arrived back at the hospital, there was no sign of Declan and she was informed that he'd finished his clinic early and had left.

Claire quickly called through to Mary, unable to raise any of her other siblings, and asked her to pass a message on to Jason that she wouldn't be home for dinner.

'You're going out with Declan, aren't you?' Mary declared, not hiding her excitement.

'Yes.'

'Go. Have a good time. Don't you worry about a thing. I'll make sure Brett studies and I'll also check on Lizzie's hand and change the dressing if necessary.'

'All the bandages are—'

'Claire, I know where the bandages are. You just go and concentrate on you for a while. Enjoy yourself and if you decide not to come home, well, I'm more than happy to drop a change of clothes off at his motel in the morning.'

'Mary!' Claire's face become hot at her sister's suggestion. 'It's dinner. It's nothing like that. Besides, even if he did invite me, which he wouldn't because he's not that kind of guy, I still wouldn't accept because I'm not that kind of girl.'

Mary chuckled. 'I know, but it was worth saying it just for your reaction.'

Claire put a hand over her eyes and shook her head. 'Don't do that to me, Mary. The man's got me in enough of a tizz as it is.'

'I'm glad you can finally admit that. I noticed it in you the first night you brought him home.'

'Everything's moving so fast, Mary. What am I supposed to do?'

'Ah, that's an easy question to answer, especially as I've been through it all myself. Remember how hard and fast I fell for Greg. You thought I was being impossibly romantic and silly.'

Claire groaned. 'I should have known you'd throw that back in my face one day.'

'Well, that day has come, big sister, and my advice to you is just let it happen. Don't fight the fall. Enjoy it. The sensation of floating on a cloud is so rare, so special and so wonderful. Embrace it. You may have been kidding yourself that you wanted peace and time to yourself but come on, Claire…really? I know you better. You believe in that one true love and you may have found him in Declan. Enjoy it because it won't happen again.'

'Enjoy it? Embrace it?' Claire opened her eyes and looked at the wall. 'What if I can't?'

Mary laughed. 'Oh, Claire, you can. I know you can. I have faith in you. Think of the wonderful paintings you'll create from this experience, how it will just pour out of you onto the canvas and how it will end up being the best work you've ever done. Just take a breath and let go.'

So she'd taken a breath and was now standing outside Declan's motel, about to enter the coffee shop. She took another calming breath, getting herself under control. She needed to be open to Declan, to be willing to listen to him as well as giving of herself in return. She knew this was a two-way street and one she wanted to travel down. But what if she crashed? What if things didn't work out? What if she let go and she got hurt?

Mary's words went through her mind once more. 'Just take a breath and let go.' Claire whispered them softly as she breathed in again and held it for a second before breathing out, mentally forcing herself to push her inhibitions and natural reserve aside. After all, Declan was worth it.

She put a bright smile on her face and pushed open the door to the coffee shop, stopping dead in her tracks, her eyes staring wide at the sight before her. Declan sat at a table, laughing joyously at a blond woman sitting opposite him.

She wanted to scream, to let her immediate pain and frustration out. Jealousy—bright, green and infections—wound its way around her heart and squeezed tight. She wanted to disappear, to become invisible so he wouldn't see her and she could slink away to heal herself in private. Instead, she froze, her hand still on the door, the smile still plastered on her face.

It was then he saw her and she knew there was no escape. If she'd thought her heart had been beating wildly before she'd entered, it was nothing compared to now. Her palms began to perspire and she wasn't sure her legs would hold her up any longer. She held his gaze for a moment, her smile slipping as she glanced at the other blonde.

No. No. She couldn't do this. She couldn't watch him smile and laugh with another woman, especially when he didn't seem to have any fear or anxiety about her. Did women always just flock to him? The nurses at the hospital were bad enough but here? Now? When she'd just realised she was in love with him? The love was so new, so fragile and right now it felt as though it was breaking...or was that her heart?

She turned slightly, knowing if only she could prise her fingers from the doorhandle she could leave, but her hand refused to co-operate.

'Claire.'

It was too late. She turned back and watched as he quickly stood and crossed to her side. 'Claire.' He took her free hand in his and gave it a squeeze. 'Come on over.'

Claire found it hard to stop the trembling but Declan was being his usual self, bright and jovial, and she knew she couldn't refuse him even though meeting the woman who had him so enthralled was the last thing she wanted to do.

'House calls run late or did Cathy keep you chatting?'

'Hmm?' She glanced up at him. They were getting closer. Closer to the table of doom. 'Er...yes.'

'You all right?'

'Uh...sure.'

'I'm sorry I couldn't stay and wait for you.'

'That's all right. We did agree to meet here and I can see you've been busy.'

'You're not wrong. I've been on a shopping spree, scoured the town for arts and crafts shops and carried a lot of bags.'

'But you don't like craft,' she whispered, more to herself than to him, but Declan merely smiled and pointed to his companion.

'This is one lady who knows how to shop!'

They'd reached the table and Declan placed his arm about her shoulders and made the introductions. 'Claire, this is my cousin, Louisa.'

His cousin! She'd been jealous of his *cousin*. Shame washed over her. She should have trusted him more but it was so hard with her emotions so wild and new and out of control.

'She's come down to do the audiologist clinic tomorrow.'

'It's really nice to meet you, Claire.'

Claire smiled politely and took the woman's hand, reassessing her initial reaction. She began to feel a little foolish but she instantly rationalised that she had only just discovered a few hours ago that she was in love with the man. How was she supposed to react to seeing him laughing happily with another woman?

Declan came and sat beside her, bringing his chair closer and placing his arm about her shoulders in a protective and possessive way. Claire could see Louisa taking everything in. They ordered drinks and chatted for a while, but then Louisa laughed and shook her head.

'What's funny?' Declan asked.

'It's just…I've never seen you like this before, Dec. Sorry Claire. I don't mean to embarrass you but he's just so…relaxed.'

Declan's grin increased and he bent and placed a kiss on Claire's cheek. 'She's good for me.'

Claire couldn't help it. She felt vulnerable and exposed. She was in love with Declan and now he was saying that she was good for him. What did that mean? She wasn't used to psychoanalysing every little word and nuance. That was Declan's territory. The longer she sat there, with Declan's arm about her shoulders, the more confused she became.

'Well, I'm bushed so I might go to my room and get some sleep,' Louisa said. 'Declan tells me I have a full clinic tomorrow and as it's my first official one, I want to make sure I'm bright-eyed and bushy-tailed.'

Declan stood and when Louisa came around the table, he hugged his cousin. 'Thanks for coming,' he said again, 'let me walk you to your room.'

'No. It's fine. It was great to meet you, Claire.' She held out her hand. 'I guess I'll see you tomorrow at the hospital.'

Claire also stood and nodded politely. She felt so mixed up, her emotions churning, she wasn't sure what to do. Once Louisa had gone, Declan turned to face her, his smile eager, his eyes alive with excitement. 'Well?'

She gave him a cool stare. 'Well, what?'

'What do you think?'

'Of what? The coffee? We can do better.'

'Claire?'

She watched as the excitement was replaced by concern and a frown. She'd done that. She'd single-handedly destroyed his mood, but at the moment it couldn't be helped. Claire clenched her teeth together, realising she was probably upset about nothing. As his expression continued to sober, she began to feel more guilty. Why couldn't she have just smiled and answered his question? Why did she have to let her confusion ruin everything? She usually did this, though. When she was upset or tired or frustrated, she would cover up her real emotions with briskness. The question now was could she trust Declan, trust this new-found love she had for him and open up? To let loose of the tight rein she held over her life? To tell Declan that she loved him? Looking into his eyes did nothing except make her melt, and she didn't want to melt.

Claire stood and gathered up her bag, clearing her throat. 'Actually, Declan, I'm not feeling too well. Do you mind if we skip dinner tonight?'

'Claire? What's wrong?'

She sighed. 'I'm tired. It's been a long day. All that standing around in Theatre, I guess.'

He shook his head. 'You're not telling me something.'

'I'm not telling you a lot of things. We hardly know each other and while there may be this attraction between us, it doesn't mean we have to jump onto the train and let it carry us away.'

Declan's frown increased at her outburst. Something was wrong, terribly wrong, but he also sensed she needed time to unravel things. To push her now would probably ruin things between them and that was the last thing he wanted to do. He nodded. 'All right. We'll take a rain check on dinner.' He purposely kept his voice light and soothing, not wanting to upset her further by saying the wrong thing. 'I'll walk you to your car.'

'No. It's fine. I can walk all by myself.'

'Please?'

The one word got to her. She knew she shouldn't let it but it did. The man had a way of making her feel special and needed and glorious and feminine and he could do it all with one simple look combined with one simple word—*please*.

'Fine.'

Fine? He'd gotten a 'fine'? Ooh, he was in a bad place. Whenever a woman said 'fine' in that tone of voice, it meant bad news or that he'd done something to upset her. Declan racked his brains, trying to think what he'd done wrong so he could apologise and fix it. Whatever it was had been done inadvertently, but from the way Claire was behaving, he doubted she was in a mood to either listen to reason or to see it. He escorted her from the motel's coffee shop out into the street. The sun had gone down and the stars were beginning to twinkle brightly in the almost cloudless, moonlit sky. It was the perfect night for walking and gazing up at the wondrous sky…but Claire's attitude said otherwise.

'Louisa didn't need your protection walking to her room,' Claire felt compelled to point out. 'I'm just going to my car.'

Again, Declan was stunned. 'Louisa has a black belt in karate. She'd kick *my* butt without breaking a sweat.'

'I'll have to get her to give me some tips, then,' she muttered, but obviously Declan heard.

'What's wrong? Come on, Claire.'

They'd reached her car and he was about to try and hold her in his arms, to kiss her, to let her know that whatever was bothering her, she wasn't alone, that he was here to help, when she groaned. At first, Declan wondered if she really was in pain. When she'd said she hadn't felt well, he'd thought she meant mentally, not physically. She didn't look sick but when he followed her gaze he realised why she'd groaned. She'd left the lights on in her car.

'Turn them off and try turning the engine over,' he suggested.

'I know what to do.'

'I didn't mean to imply otherwise.' It didn't seem to matter *what* he said, it was going to be the wrong thing. When she tried to start the engine, it gave nothing but a click. 'It's dead.' Her annoyance with herself grew. How could she have made such a stupid mistake?

'We could push it,' Declan suggested. 'Jump-start it that way.'

'It's an automatic.'

'Oh.'

'You don't have jump-leads, by any chance?'

'No. Sorry.'

'And all the shops and the garage have closed down for the night.'

'There's isn't a twenty-four-hour petrol station open?'

'On the outskirts of town in the opposite direction.' Claire sighed heavily and pulled out her cell phone. 'I'll have to get one of my siblings to come pick me up.'

Declan reached out and put his hand over hers. 'Let me drive you home, Claire.'

'It's all right. Thomas can come.'

'Claire, they'll be sitting down to their dinner soon. There's no need to disturb them when I'm more than happy to offer my services. I'll even keep quiet on the drive and not ask you a single question.' That broke the drought and he received a small smile for his efforts…a very small smile. 'We can sort your car out tomorrow.'

The weariness was really starting to set in and she could feel her mind beginning to shut down. What she'd said to Declan earlier had been an excuse to leave but now the busyness of the day, the theatre stint, the house calls, realising she was in love with him—*everything*—seemed to swamp her and she was too tired to even argue with him.

'OK.'

'Better than "fine",' he mumbled.

'Pardon?'

'Nothing. Nothing at all,' he said as he helped her from her car. Taking her hand in his, he led her to where his car was parked in the motel car park. 'I'm zipping my lips.'

'But holding my hand is all right, eh?'

'I said I'd keep quiet. I didn't say I wouldn't touch you.' He stopped at his car and opened the passenger door for her. 'There you are, m'lady.'

Claire glanced up at him. 'This is you keeping quiet?'

Before she could get into the car, he brushed his lips over hers then nodded, miming the motions of zipping, buttoning and even sewing his lips together, pretending to tug on the imaginary suture. Claire couldn't help but smile at the childish but completely heart-melting gesture. She climbed in and he closed the door before heading around to the driver's side.

True to his word, he didn't speak but wherever possible, when he wasn't changing gears, he held her hand. He glanced at her a few times, wondering whether she was going to tell him what he'd done wrong, but as she had her head back and eyes closed, he doubted that was possible. He just wished he knew what he'd done so he could fix it. He didn't like being at odds with Claire. The woman was extremely important to him and while he'd heard her when she'd said she wasn't interested in long-term relationships, he couldn't help but hope she might change her mind…or that she'd at least let him help her change it.

He prided himself on being open and honest but he knew if he were honest about his feelings for her, he'd scare her away for good. He knew he was falling for her, and in a big way, but he couldn't help the way he felt. Being true and honest to his own feelings was something he'd learnt to do many years ago as it helped him deal with the anxiety. Also, if Claire couldn't tell him what he'd done, he'd spend another restless night trying to figure it out. He needed to get back to Brisbane just so he could catch up on his sleep because since he'd arrived in Mt Black, Claire Neilson had tied him up in knots.

Declan glanced across at her. She looked so at peace, resting the cares of her day away. When he returned his attention to the road, he slammed on the brakes as he noticed a man in the middle of the road, trying to flag him down.

Claire was instantly alert as she was jerked forward. 'Declan? What's going on?' There was mild panic in her tone.

'There.' He pointed and then she saw the man stepping to the side of the road, where his car was parked.

'That's Benjamin Tuttle's old car. Pull over.'

'You know him?' Declan continued to decrease speed, although not as dramatically, and stopped not far from the other car. He quickly reversed, bringing them closer.

'Ben's wife, Minnie, is pregnant. I saw her last week in my clinic.'

'You think we've got an emergency on our hands?'

'By the way Benjamin was frantically standing in the middle of the road, trying to flag someone down, I'd say that's a big yes.'

As soon as Declan stopped the car, Claire climbed out and rushed towards Ben.

'Oh, Dr Claire. I'm so glad it's you.' Ben fell on her with relief. 'It's Minnie.' He indicated the station wagon. 'She's in labour and I was bringing her in, but the car broke down.'

'Seems to be the season,' she mumbled, as she raced over to the station wagon.

'I put her in the back,' Ben said. 'I know it's not the safest but she had trouble sitting down in the front seat. Said she needed more room.'

'It's fine, Ben.' The tailgate door was open and Claire ducked beneath it. 'Hey there, Minnie.'

'Oh, Dr Claire.' The stress seemed to melt away from the woman as she saw the face of her doctor. 'I'm so glad it's you. Oh, my Ben. He always gets me the moon.'

'How far apart are the contractions?'

'Two minutes.'

Declan came over, carrying his medical bag.

'Have your waters broken?'

'Yes. That's why we thought we'd better come to the hospital, except ol' Tracer here decided now was a good time not to work.'

'Tracer?' Declan asked.

'The car,' Claire explained. 'All right. We'll see if we can get you into the back of Declan's car and get you to the hospital.'

Minnie's face pinched as another contraction made itself known.

'Or maybe we can leave you where you are and deliver a

baby,' Claire continued. 'Declan, bring your car around so the headlights are shining in here. That should give us more light.'

'It's going to be OK, isn't it, Dr Claire?' Ben asked, wringing his hands.

Claire smiled at Ben. 'Everything's going to be fine. The baby's the right way around, Minnie's gone to full term and I've done this before. Don't panic.'

While Declan did as Claire had asked, she pulled on a pair of gloves and did an internal check. 'You're fully dilated, Minnie.'

'I want to push,' Minnie panted.

'Then push. Remember your breathing.'

Declan was back before the contraction finished. 'I've called the hospital and notified Night Sister. She's going to send Cathy with the ambulance.'

'Good.' She glanced at him and smiled. 'Ever delivered a baby before?'

'This is the first one I've done in the middle of the road.' Claire grinned.

'What do I do?' Ben asked, still standing on the side of the road.

'Why don't you come and get into the back seat?' Declan suggested. 'That way, you'll be behind Minnie and able to rub her back or have the life squeezed out of your hand if necessary.'

Ben glanced down at his hands and then nodded. 'Anything for my Min.'

When the next contraction came, Claire was ready for it. 'The head's crowning,' she said. 'Keep it up, Minnie. You're doing a brilliant job.'

Declan looked around for blankets, going to his car and hoisting some from the boot. It was the rule, when driving in rural parts of Australia, to carry extra fuel, extra water and blankets, in case of fires. 'Or emergency births,' he said softly to himself as he rushed back to Claire's side. He looked into his medical bag and found a pair of scissors but couldn't find anything to tie off the umbilical cord with.

'What are you looking for?' Claire asked when Minnie was between contractions.

'Something for the cord.'

'Ben? Got any rope?'

'Yep. I shifted it into the back seat to get it out of Minnie's way. It's just all-purpose rope, one quarter of an inch thick. It's orange.'

'That will do perfectly,' Claire told him with a smile, and Ben handed it to Declan. 'Cut off a few pieces,' she instructed, and Declan followed orders. When Minnie gave the next big push, the head was finally out.

'Right. Now we wait for the shoulders to rotate and then it won't be long until it's over. You're doing a fantastic job. Keep it up.' Claire checked the baby's neck and was pleased the cord wasn't wrapped around it. 'All clear,' she said to Declan.

'Good.'

'You want to catch it?' Claire asked, and Declan raised his eyebrows with delight.

'Can I?'

'I've done plenty. Minnie? Do you mind if—?'

'I don't care. Just get it out!' Minnie groaned as another contraction ripped through her body.

Declan supported the head and reached a hand around as Minnie pushed. The shoulders were out.

'Keep pushing,' Claire and Declan said in unison.

'That's it. That's my Minnie,' Ben encouraged. Minnie clenched her jaw, dragged in a breath and pushed. The result was a healthy baby boy slipping out into Declan's large, capable hands. Claire worked quickly, tying the rope and giving the scissors to Ben, who leaned over to cut the cord. Then she quickly cleaned out the nose and mouth as best she could while Declan rubbed his gloved fingers over the baby's chest.

'Come on, little one,' he encouraged.

'Let me have him,' Claire said, and she picked him up and tickled his feet, before checking the baby's mouth for mucus. An instant later the baby dragged in a breath and cried. Claire wrapped him in one of the large blankets Declan had brought over and handed him to his mother.

'Here he is,' she said. 'Your very beautiful little boy.'

Minnie and Ben were amazed and enthralled and while they cooed at the newest addition to their family, Declan stared at Claire.

'You're amazing,' he said softly, and couldn't help but kiss her. Thankfully, she let him. 'You knew exactly what to do and you had no equipment.'

Claire laughed. 'Babies have always been born, Declan. Sometimes the old-fashioned way is the best.' She looked at their surroundings. 'Especially when there's no other option.'

Minnie yawned. 'Can someone take him, please?'

'Yes.' Claire took the baby and handed him to Declan. 'I'll take care of the next stage of labour. You look after this one.'

'With pleasure.' He looked down at the wee babe in his arms, unable to believe the miracle of life. This wasn't the first baby he'd delivered but it was the first one he'd done outside a hospital where every piece of machinery had been at his disposal had he needed it. Out here, beneath the starry sky, it seemed not only scary but incredibly perfect. It was such a contradiction but a contradiction that made sense.

Cathy arrived with the ambulance and helped Ben get Minnie onto the stretcher. Claire took a moment and sat on the edge of the tailgate and sighed.

'You were brilliant,' Declan murmured. 'Just brilliant.'

Claire looked at him, standing there in the beam of light, holding a tiny, tiny baby. It was a dangerous picture to witness and she immediately knew this was one scene she'd definitely paint. He would make such a wonderful father, she was sure of it, and she already knew she'd make a great mother...she had the siblings to prove it.

Could it work? Could she have a life with Declan? What about her family? Although Jason and Elizabeth, as well as Thomas, were all over the official age of consent, they still needed her and she needed them. Brett would soon join their ranks but he, too, would still need her. Eighteen seemed so young to be called an adult but that was the way it was. It was nice to be needed by her family but in the past few days she'd come to realise that it wasn't enough. But what man in his right mind would want to take on an instant family?

Declan would, came the immediate answer, and she knew it to be true. Yes, she was in danger. Very grave danger.

CHAPTER TEN

FINALLY, they were able to move the Tuttle family to a more suitable location. Night Sister was more than happy to receive the new family and fussed over them accordingly.

'He's just perfectly made,' Claire told Minnie.

'Oh, Claire, I don't know what I would have done without you and Dr Silvermark. It was a blessing you came along when you did.'

Claire smiled at Minnie, kissed the little boy's downy head and glanced up at Declan, who had just walked into the room.

'There you are,' Minnie said. 'I was just saying to Claire how grateful we are. I don't know how to thank you. Words don't seem enough.'

Declan smiled and rubbed his finger across the baby's cheek. 'Be the best parents you can be. That's the best way to thank us— oh, and tell the story of his delivery over and over again so it can be passed down from generation to generation.'

'Hoping to immortalise yourself in history, Declan?' Claire asked.

'Absolutely.' He smiled brightly and Claire reached a hand out to the bed to steady herself. The picture of him holding the baby still remained and she knew it would be burned onto her memory for ever.

She broke her gaze from his and cleared her throat. 'So...' Her voice was shaky but she pressed on, cross with Declan for inadvertently affecting her. 'What are you going to call him?'

Minnie looked lovingly at her husband and then down at her son, who was still sleeping peacefully in her arms. 'We haven't decided. We had a girl's name all picked out but not a boy's.'

Claire chuckled. 'Always the way. Well, I look forward to learning his name when you eventually decide.'

'It won't be too long,' Minnie said, and gave her husband a look. Declan knew what it meant. Minnie was determined to get her way and after everything she'd been through tonight, Ben was bound to give in. Declan glanced at Claire and realised she'd caught the same moment.

'We'd better get going,' they said in unison, and then laughed.

'You're doing great,' Claire told Minnie. 'And despite this little one's impatience to get here, he's doing well, too.' She glanced at Ben. 'Once Sister makes up the camp-bed, you're to get as much sleep as you can. In fact, both of you should be resting if nothing else. You'll soon learn, when the baby's asleep—*you* sleep.'

'I'm just too wired,' Minnie said, and Claire nodded.

'That's common.' She walked towards the door and Declan followed. 'Remember, if you need any help, buzz through to Sister. She'd only be too happy to have a cuddle with that little tacker. The midwife will be around first thing in the morning to see you, and as everyone is happy and healthy, Declan's going to take me home to bed.' Claire's eyes widened as she realised what she'd said. 'Er...he's going to drive me home,' she added quickly, trying to clarify it. 'And I'll be with all my siblings and then I'll go to my room, to bed, alone.'

Minnie chuckled. 'You're digging yourself in deeper.'

Declan didn't join in the laughter but instead continued out the room. Even just thinking about escorting Claire up to her bedroom gave him palpitations. What was he supposed to do? The woman tied him up in knots, drove him crazy and senseless to the point of total frustration, and then threw out comments like that! No wonder he was anxious about loving her. He had every right to be.

They quickly did a check on their other patients before saying goodnight to Sister and heading out to the car. 'I…er…didn't mean what I just said. It came out the wrong way.'

'It's fine,' he said with a forced smile. He held the door for her and once she was safely inside, he slowly walked around the rear of the car, forcing himself to take deep breaths and get himself under control. What was a man supposed to do when comments like that brought vivid pictures to mind? He was flesh and blood. He wanted her, there was no doubt about that, but he also wanted to do right by her. She was the type of woman who deserved the best, and he'd often wondered in the last few days whether that was him. Was he the right man for Claire? He didn't know if he could answer that, but what he could answer was that the thought of Claire with any other man made him wild with jealousy.

Knowing he couldn't stall any longer, he opened the driver's door and climbed in, clipping his seat belt into place before starting the engine. As with their previous drive out to her place, neither of them spoke and this time Declan made no move to hold her hand, either. Everything she did, the way she had cared not just for Minnie but for Ben as well, the way she'd delivered that baby like a pro, the way she'd coped with being in the middle of nowhere with no medical support…

The woman was amazing. The vision he had of her, cradling the newborn babe in her arms as she'd looked down at the miracle of life, was one he knew he'd never tire of recalling. He glanced across at her. Claire. *His* Claire. It was the way he'd thought of her for days now and he knew that would never change. She was the woman for him. He'd accepted that, realised he'd never stop loving her, whatever happened between them.

He knew he had to move forward but taking a big step into uncharted territory terrified him. From the first day he'd met her, Claire had always been the reluctant one, reluctant to get involved with him. That had forced him into the position of the pursuer and he'd coped well with that. He loved teasing her, seeing that little flash of fighting-furious glint in her brown eyes before she realised he was only pulling her leg.

It was the little things, he realised. Just those personalised little things that had made him fall in love with her. The way she'd placed her hand on Brett's shoulder in support, how she'd encouraged Thomas, praised Jason, cared for Elizabeth and looked to Mary for advice. Declan was sure she'd had no idea he'd been watching her so closely, but he had and he'd become…entranced.

When he pulled into her driveway, she spoke, making him jump. 'Sorry,' he said, chuckling, feeling some of the tension leave him. 'I was miles away.'

'I'd like to apologise for my behaviour earlier.'

'When?' Declan frowned.

'When I met Louisa.'

'That's all right. I probably shouldn't have sprung it on you the way I did. I know I don't like surprises but it often doesn't occur to me to think other people are like that.'

'So used to being unique?'

He laughed again. 'I guess. Sounds a bit egotistical.'

'It's understandable.' She paused. 'You're right, though. I don't like surprises. I need to be prepared, to have an understanding of what's going on and what's expected of me in certain circumstances.' Claire looked down at her hands and clasped her fingers together. 'I guess with what I've had to deal with since my parents' deaths, I need things to be orderly.'

Declan nodded. 'You and I are more alike than we'd initially thought, although we both have different reasons for why we are the way we are.'

'You're academically gifted and I became an orphan at eighteen. Can't get more different than that.'

Declan reached over and took her hands in his before gazing into her eyes. Even though the light was dim, he could see her. It was intuitive—their hearts and souls connected on a level only the two of them could reach. 'I'm sorry about your parents, Claire.' His words were deep, sincere and she felt tears prick behind her eyes. 'I wish I'd been able to know them because they sound like such wonderful people.'

She swallowed over the lump in her throat and nodded. 'They were. They were.' He lifted one hand to caress her cheek.

'It must have been so hard for you, holding yourself in check all these years, not giving yourself the chance at a real life.

You've put everyone else first and that's not only honourable, it's admirable and I love that about you.'

'You…' She stared at him, unsure if he'd just said what she'd thought he'd said. Had he really said he loved her or had he just been making a comment about her inner strength? 'Did you just…?' she tried again, but couldn't get her tongue around the words. A wave of heat swamped her and her skin began to prickle. She edged back, pulling her hands from his and shifting so he would stop caressing her cheek.

'What's wrong?' he asked, trying to read her, interpret her. She was the most baffling female he'd ever come across and he was in love with her.

'Nothing.' Claire shook her head, telling herself she'd imagined the whole thing. 'I need to go inside.' She gathered her things and was out of the car like a shot.

'Claire?' Declan moved equally as fast and cornered her just short of the sensor light, his hands on her shoulders. 'Claire, stop. Wait a minute.'

'What? What is it, Declan?'

'That was my question…except I was going to put "Claire" on the end, rather than my own name.'

She looked away. 'Stop being so cute. You're only making this more difficult.'

'What? What am I making more difficult?'

Claire found it hard to meet his gaze.

'Please?' he implored softly, and slowly slid his hands down her arms. 'Let me inside your head, Claire. Let me know what's going on.'

Claire swallowed. She was definitely in uncharted territory but, then, so was Declan…wasn't he? He'd opened up to her and she had opened up to him—more so than she'd done with any other man. Admittedly, they'd both only allowed each other access to a certain point. Self-preservation was a hard habit to break but wasn't he worth it? This…*thing* between them was worth it, wasn't it?

She raised her gaze to meet his. 'This isn't easy for me.'

'I know,' he encouraged. 'Or for me, either.'

'Declan…' Claire sighed and shook her head, knowing the best way to say what she needed to was to do it quickly. 'Declan…'

'We got that far last time.'

Claire frowned at him and stamped her foot. 'Stop teasing me. This isn't funny, you know. It's downright hard to tell someone you love them and you're not making it easy for me.' She watched as his expression changed to one of shock. 'Oops.' She covered her mouth. 'I didn't mean for it to… Oh, forget it.' She turned to go but once more Declan stopped her.

'No. Don't.' He looked at her and swallowed over the dryness of his throat. 'You know I feel the same way, right?' Oh, smooth, Silvermark. Real smooth. He cringed as he heard the words come out. In one way he felt as though she'd handed him the world, and in another way a ticking time bomb. One second his heart sang with joy and the next it constricted so tightly he thought he might pass out. He could feel beads of sweat break out on his brow. He knew as she'd said the words out loud, it was only fair that he follow suit. After all, it was true. He did love her but knowing you loved a woman and telling her were two different things. Then again, he wasn't about to let fear or anxiety stop him from doing what he needed to do. 'That didn't come out right.'

Claire smiled shyly. 'And you think mine did?'

He returned her smile and suddenly a huge weight lifted from his shoulders. 'I love you, Claire. I've known you for less than a week but there it is. I can't help it, I can't stop it and neither do I want to.'

'It's scary.'

'Terrifying.'

She gave him a playful thump. 'Not *that* terrifying.'

He chuckled and gathered her close, resting his chin on her head. Claire closed her eyes and rested her head against his chest, loving the sound of his heart—a heart that was beating with love for her.

'So what do we do?' she murmured.

'I have no idea. This is all so…sudden.'

'Yes,' she agreed.

'New.'

'Definitely.'

'Life altering.'

'All right, all right. I get the drift,' she joked.

'Sorry. It's just I find it fascinating the way one minute you think you have control over your life and then, *bam*, something happens to blow all your careful plans out of the water.'

'So now I'm like a bomb?'

'A love bomb?' he tried.

'Corny, but I'll let it pass.'

Declan looked down at her. 'Seriously, Claire, what do we do now?'

'I think we need some space. Some time to think. To sort out what's going to happen.'

'I guess this is kind of difficult for you, especially as you've always said you weren't interested in a relationship. And I want you to know,' he rushed on when she opened her mouth to defend herself, 'that I completely understand that. It's a big change in how you thought your life would turn out. I, on the other hand, always knew one day I'd meet the most extraordinary woman on the face of this earth and hoped she'd feel the same about me. I'd love to marry you, to have children with you and I can see by the terrified look on your face that I'm moving things faster than you'd thought but I guess that's the way I am. Once I get over the anxiety and find my confidence, it's full steam ahead. I know you wanted peace and solitude, Claire, but you're such a vibrant, giving woman that you'd be bored within a month of having that wish come true.'

'Declan, I just need some—'

'Time. I know. I understand. I'll be back in Brisbane in a couple of days so that should give us both some breathing space. Although I will need to stay in contact. Can I call you? Email you?'

Claire wasn't sure it was such a good idea but neither was she sure she could go cold turkey. Declan had erupted into her life, turning it upside down, as he'd previously said, and not to speak to him or have any contact with him might be worse for her peace of mind. He'd become such an integral part of her life, part of her being, and she wasn't sure she could cut him out even if she'd wanted to.

'Sure.' She nodded.

'You don't sound too positive.'

'No. It'll be fine.'

'I also need to check up on Brett, too, and I don't want to have to use him as an excuse just to call you.'

'Would you have?'

'In a heartbeat if you'd said no.'

Claire shook her head. 'I'm still getting used to this honesty thing from a man, you know.'

Declan chuckled and bent his head to kiss her. 'Then let's start getting you used to other things.'

When his lips found hers, when they touched with the promise of love and the growing familiarity between them, he knew this woman belonged to him. It was primal, it was Neanderthal, but it was the way he felt. The opposite was also true. He belonged to her and that gave him such a feeling of peace, a feeling of homecoming, and he knew it would be for ever.

The kiss they shared was different to all the others. This one was unique, it was special, it was filled with love, and he knew that alone would help him through the separation they were about to endure.

Claire didn't hold back. There was no need now. She'd told him she loved him and it had taken away a lot of her stress. His mouth was so perfect for hers and she couldn't get enough of him. She grabbed the lapels of his coat and urged him closer before winding her arms about his neck, her fingers lacing themselves into his hair.

When he moaned in delight, an amazing feminine rush washed over her. She liked the power she had over him. It made her feel strong and unbreakable while at the same time she knew he held a similar power over her. There was an equal amount of give and take and she wondered whether anyone else on the planet had ever felt the way she did right now.

His scent was so much a part of her. She loved it, knowing it would always remind her of him and would bring a need that would continue to grow for the rest of her life. He was hers. For ever. Nothing and no one was going to take that away from her. She'd fight tooth and nail for him and the fierceness of her emotions came as quite a shock.

Claire pulled back, her breath coming out in little puffs of steam in the cool night air. Her eyes were wide as she gazed up at him, not trying to hide what she was feeling.

'What is it?' he breathed, looking at her with a mixture of passion and concern.

'I just feel so…' She shook her head. 'This love… It's just so…'

'Big?'

'*Yes.*'

'Overwhelming?'

'Yes.'

'Consuming.'

'Yes, oh, yes. You feel it, too?'

'I do.' Declan placed a kiss on her cold nose. 'You're not in this alone, Claire. This new discovery. It's the two of us. You and me. Together.'

She chuckled, loving the way he became all logical when he was flustered. 'Can you say that another way? I didn't get the picture.'

'Stop teasing. That's my job.'

'Says who?'

'Says me. Read the fine print.'

'Fine print on what?'

'On the courtship documents.'

'Courtship?'

'Isn't that what we're doing? Courting?'

Claire smiled, loving his old-fashioned manner, his chivalry. 'I guess it is.'

'Well, then, as your suitor…' He raised his eyebrows and smiled at the word. 'I'd suggest you go inside as it's getting cooler.'

'I could be coy and say, "Well, I have you to warm me up," but—'

'But you're anything but coy.'

'I could be coy, if I tried.'

Declan shook his head. 'I prefer genuine and you're definitely that, my darling Claire.' He pressed three quick kisses to her luscious lips before putting her from him. 'Inside, get warm and off to sleep. It's been an…eventful night.'

'In more ways than one.' Claire backed towards the door, blinking rapidly as the sensor light came on. 'I'll see you tomorrow.'

'Yes.'

'Drive carefully.'

'I will.'

'Call me when you get to the motel.' The words blurted out before she could stop them. 'Just so I know you're all right,' she added.

Declan nodded, understanding her need. 'Of course.' Knowing he was going to speak to her soon helped him to walk to his car and get in. He waved as he drove off, eager to get back to the motel just so he could hear her voice again but knowing he had to concentrate on the road. They'd already had one emergency tonight and they didn't need another one.

Finally, he drove into the parking space and climbed from the car, locking it before entering his room. After closing the door and throwing his room key onto the desk, he walked to the phone and called Claire's home number.

'You're there already?' she said.

'Hello to you, too.'

'Did you speed?'

'I may have done a little over the speed limit from time to time but for the most part, no.'

Claire paused. 'I'm sorry, Declan. I don't mean to nag.'

'It's fine. I understand, Claire. I'm here. I'm fine.' He lay down on the bed and kicked off his shoes. 'Where are you? All snuggled up?'

'Yes.'

'Good.' He voice broke on the word and he quickly cleared his throat. His mind could easily paint a vivid picture of exactly where she was and what she was wearing. Whether he was accurate or not, he didn't care. She was his Claire and he loved feeling he had permission to dream about her.

'I won't keep you,' she said, and Declan could hear the huskiness in her tone. Was she thinking what he was thinking? 'Thank you for calling. I've worried about you every time you've left here, wondering whether you'd arrived safely or not.'

Declan was touched. 'Well, you can rest assured tonight that I am here and I am safe.'

'I'm glad.' There was an awkward pause for a moment before she reiterated, 'I won't keep you.'

'I hope you do,' he couldn't resist teasing softly, and loved it when she giggled.

'I didn't mean it that way, you dolt.'

'I know. Sleep sweet, Claire.'

'I will. You, too. I'll see you tomorrow.'

Declan replaced the receiver, wondering exactly what tomorrow would bring. She'd said she needed space and tomorrow was his last day here. Once he'd finished his hospital work in the afternoon, his services would no longer be required at Mt Black Hospital until it was time for next month's clinic. Did she want to be apart the whole time? He wasn't sure he could handle it but at the moment he needed to give her whatever space she wanted. He only hoped she wouldn't keep him waiting too long. Honest he might be but patient he was not.

Claire wasn't sure how she managed to get through Declan's last day at the clinic but she did. From the moment she'd woken up in the morning to the moment she knew he had to leave, there had been a dark cloud over her. Twice she'd picked a quarrel with him and twice he'd let her. Then she'd got mad with his pacifying attitude and had stormed off. Thankfully, he seemed to understand her mood and hadn't pushed her on it. He was amazingly perfect for her and those incidents alone proved that.

Now, though, she could hear him packing up in the clinic room next to her. It was late and everyone else had left the clinic area. It was just the two of them, the way she'd wanted it to be all day long but instead she'd had to share him with Louisa and the patients and the staff, not to mention her own siblings who'd dropped in to say their own goodbyes during the day.

She continued to put things away, tidying the room unnecessarily, knowing she was stalling actually facing the moment he would leave but knowing it would come nevertheless. How could one man have made such a difference in her life in such a short time? It was a question she'd been asking herself all week long as Declan had become more important to her. Surely she wasn't really in love with him? Was she?

Claire slumped into the chair and buried her head in her hands, whimpering a little at her lack of control. She'd always been in control. From the moment her parents had died, leaving her responsible and in charge of her family, she'd been in control. During her struggle through medical school, trying to juggle everything successfully, she'd remained in control. Even when she'd dated Ken, *she* had been the one calling the shots, making the decisions about how fast the relationship would progress. She'd been in control.

With Declan, that control had gone out the window from the first time she'd seen him. She smiled to herself, recalling the brilliant way he'd dealt with little Pierce Cameron. Both she and Declan had been there when Louisa had performed her audiology tests on the young four-year-old and again Claire was impressed with Declan's holistic approach to medicine. It wasn't often she found that with the specialists who did their week-long clinics here in Mt Black. Most of them just came, did their jobs and left, not caring or wanting to know who their patients really were.

To Declan, Pierce Cameron was more than file number 2912. He was a boy who needed help, who was now getting that help thanks to the correct diagnosis. Declan had treated all his patients with the same congeniality, wanting to get to know them, to form relationships with them, and she knew her patients would be eagerly awaiting the return of the new ENT specialist next month. Together they'd worked through the files and Claire now had about six patients she needed to catch up with, just to check

Dr Bean had indeed prescribed the right treatment for them. Declan had possibly saved the hospital millions in legal claims.

She leaned back in the chair and started pulling her hair from the ponytail she usually wore to the clinic. Running her fingers through the strands, she managed to get most of the knots out and wished she could get the knots out of her trapezius just as easily.

It had been a hectic and arduous day and the last thing Declan needed was the sight of her with her head titled back, her eyes closed, running her fingers through her silky, golden locks while revealing the satiny curve of her neck…a neck he was desperate to nuzzle, to press his lips against.

He leaned against the doorjamb, unsure he could move but desperate to go to her at the same time. This woman had spent the entire week tying him up in knots, both physically and emotionally. He was glad he was going to his parents' house for the weekend rather than back to his lonely apartment in Brisbane. Hopefully, then he'd be able to get some sleep, even though he knew he was probably kidding himself. He would never stop thinking about Claire. She'd impacted his life in such a way he doubted even the golf game he was due to play with his father tomorrow would drive her from his thoughts.

It was getting late and although he didn't want to leave, he knew he had to. It would take him close to four hours to drive to the Gold Coast and after the busy day he'd had, he didn't want to risk an accident by leaving too late.

Without moving, Declan cleared his throat, announcing his presence. Instantly, she stopped what she was doing, sat up straight in the chair and opened her eyes. When her gaze met his, he felt himself drown in those chocolate-brown depths and knew leaving her would be almost impossible.

Claire looked down at the briefcase at his feet, then back to him. 'Ready?' Her voice broke on the word and she felt a bubble of hysteria rise up and threaten to choke her. Swallowing, she forced her mind to co-operate with her body and stood, pushing the chair in and straightening the blotter on the desk.

'Yes.'

Neither of them moved. Claire seemed highly uncomfortable, unable to meet his gaze for long, her hands always busy, tidying up and fiddling with things. Declan wasn't sure whether to simply pull her into his arms and kiss her senseless or whether to just pick up his briefcase and walk away.

The first option would be more enjoyable but possibly cause more pain in the long run. The latter would make the break sharp and clean. Finally, Claire looked at him and in that moment Declan made his decision and stalked across the room, scooping her up into his arms and pressing his mouth to hers in one swift motion.

Claire melted against him, eager to show just how much she loved him and how much she was going to miss him. She didn't want him to go but she knew he had to.

'Why is doing the grown-up thing so difficult?' she murmured against his mouth.

'I know,' he whispered, unable to let go. 'I love you, Claire.'

'I'm going to miss you and that scares me,' she said, closing her eyes, her mouth finding his easily.

'I know. I know,' he said again, and with a heart-wrenching groan, he put her from him, turned, picked up his briefcase and walked away. She knew he wouldn't look back and he didn't. Claire stood where she was until she heard the outside door of the clinic close. Even then she didn't move, *couldn't* move. How could someone possibly move when their heart was being torn in two?

She stood there, letting it happen, feeling it happen. Declan had left. In another moment, his car would leave the car park and he'd be gone. She wouldn't see him until next month when he returned for his clinic, and it was as though someone had asked her to crawl through the desert for a month with the promise of the most delicious and life-fulfilling drink at the end. She would do it, she realised. Without thought or hesitation. She would wait for him. She'd be there for him when he returned and she would live that week as though it were her last. She would spend every spare moment with him, desperate to figure out how they could be together for ever.

She *wanted* to be with him. No. She *needed* to be with him.

She'd asked him for time, time to get her head together, but she'd had no idea that just by watching him walk away from her, she'd figure everything out in the blink of an eye. For the first time in her entire life, everything became crystal clear.

She may have wanted to live a nice quiet life, to watch her siblings marry and settle down and start families of their own. She may have wanted to have just her work and her painting, telling herself that that would be enough, that she'd be content, and she'd honestly believed she would have been.

But why live a life of mere contentment when she could live a life of fulfilment—fulfilment she received through Declan and the love he professed for her?

For the next two weeks Claire's family learned to be cautious when around their big sister. Sometimes she'd be staring off into space when they were talking to her and other times she was more impatient than she'd ever been.

She spent fewer hours at work and a lot down in the barn, painting and trying to sort herself out. One minute she was determined to break it off with Declan, to get some sort of order back into her life, and the next she would give in to temptation and call him on the phone.

They talked most evenings and sometimes even chatted on-line, once Brett had showed her how to use the instant message service. Tonight it was the end of the second week since he'd walked away from her and she was relaxing after a rather busy clinic, painting while talking to him using the speaker-phone.

'Dwight Peterson came to see me today,' she said as she mixed dark blue with a bit of white, trying to find the exact shade of Declan's eyes.

'Ol' Dwight. How's he doing?'

'Much better. Thanks to you, he can actually still hear. He'll need to wear a hearing aid to assist him but he can hear and he's thrilled.'

'Glad to hear it.'

She chuckled at his bad pun. 'What about you? Busy day?'

'I was in Theatre for most of it.' His voice was tired.

'Rough time?'

'You could say that. Patient suffered a myocardial infarction near the end of the operation. We couldn't revive him.'

'Oh, Declan.' Claire glanced at the phone, wishing he was closer, wishing she could just put her arms around him and offer the comfort she knew he needed.

'Yeah. Well.' He cleared his throat. 'There is something else I wanted to talk to you about.'

'And that is?'

'There's a conference on at the Gold Coast—a GP refresher course—and I think you should attend.'

'Are you saying my GP skills need refreshing?'

'No. I'm saying you need a break and as I can't seem to persuade you to just have a holiday I thought maybe getting you to a conference might do the trick. It's only for three days and the hospital should be able to cover the time you'd need to take off.'

Claire sighed.

'What's going on, Claire?'

'Nothing.'

'You just sigh like that for nothing?'

She shook her head. 'It's just I can't be bothered going another round with the hospital board, trying to get it sorted out. The rosters will need changing, I'd be the one doing all the leg work, contacting the other GPs in town to see if they were free to cover my shifts. The clinics are booked solid for the next three weeks. I have specialists coming in and—'

'It's three days, Claire. Friday, Saturday and Sunday. You don't have any clinics on Saturdays and Sundays so it would only be the on-call roster that would require changing and then someone to do your clinic on the Friday.'

'You're not going to let up on this, are you.'

'What do you think?'

Claire sighed again.

'Look, I know you want to do more for your patients. Think of this course as an investment. You're practically more of a physician than a GP. You've certainly done the hours as well as the extra study. Doing a few of these courses will look great on your résumé when you apply to the university.'

'And why am I doing that again?'

'To become a qualified physician. Isn't that what you want?'

'All I want is peace and quiet.'

'No, you don't.'

Claire pointed a paintbrush at the phone. 'Don't tell me what I want and don't want, Declan Silvermark.' To her chagrin, he chuckled, the sound washing over her and warming her insides, melting away her annoyance. She frowned, knowing he was right.

'Sorry.'

'You are not.'

'Yes, I am,' he implored. 'I didn't mean to imply—'

'You didn't imply, you stated outright.'

'All right. I didn't mean to state outright that you don't want peace and quiet in your life. Of course you do. We all want peace and quiet...just not all the time.' He paused. 'Am I right?'

'I guess.' Claire poked her tongue out at the phone. 'Anyway, as I said, it's all too much to organise.'

'What if someone else organised it for you?'

'Well, who would do tha—' She stopped, her eyes widening as dawning realisation hit her. Her voice was soft and deadly quiet when she said, 'Tell me you didn't.'

'The conference starts next Friday. You leave on Thursday night and I'll meet you at Coolangatta airport.'

'Airport?'

'Your accommodation has been taken care of and so has the hospital board. They really need to start appreciating you more, Claire.'

'And I suppose you're going to make them?'

'You're angry. I don't blame you. If someone had organised my life the way I've done yours, I'd be spitting chips...or paint-brushes. How's the painting coming on?'

'Fine. I'm thinking of colouring a few of your teeth black, giving you a receding hairline and a lot more wrinkles.'

He chuckled. 'Laugh lines, thank you very much.'

'Wrinkles,' she said with determination.

'Does this mean you'll come?'

'Do I have a choice?'

'Of course you do.' His tone was serious, all joking gone. 'I can undo everything if you say the word, Claire.'

'Wait a minute. *You'll* pick me up from the airport?'

'Yes.'

'You'll be in the Gold Coast?'

'I'm one of the speakers at the conference.'

'Of course you are. Because you're a genius. Mr High IQ.'

Declan smiled into the phone, liking that she teased him about it. Most of the time he was very sensitive about his intellect, especially since he'd shifted to Brisbane. He was still being treated as a novelty and, quite frankly, it was wearing thin. Then again, he had other plans up his sleeve. He just hoped Claire would agree. First things first, though.

'That's right, I am, so stop arguing with me.'

'So any argument I can come up with, you'll have a counter-argument?'

'What do you think?'

'I think you like to pacify me into making me think I'm just as smart as you.'

'You are. Do you think I'm attracted to you just for your looks? Uh-uh, honey. It's your brains I love the most.'

'Gee, thanks. You really know how to sweep a girl off her feet.' Claire put her brushes to soak and decided to call it a night.

Declan chuckled. 'Come to the conference and I'll really sweep you off your feet.'

'What about the kids?'

'The *kids* are old enough to look after themselves.'

Claire paused. 'Have you spoken to any of them about this?'

'What do you think?'

'I think you have. Who? Mary? It was Mary.' Claire nodded, not waiting for confirmation from Declan. 'She was looking at me strangely when she dropped in this evening. She asked if I'd spoken to you. I don't like being organised or surprised, Declan.'

'I know. That's why I'm telling you.'

'Telling me after you've organised things.'

'I know you don't like being out of control and—'

'You've got that straight.' She stormed over to the phone and glared at the speaker box. 'Have a nice week, Declan. Good night.' She pressed the button to disconnect them.

Declan stared at the receiver and nodded firmly. 'Well, that went well.'

For the rest of the week, he concentrated on his work and the rest of the plans he was making. He still called Claire and although they spoke of general topics, neither of them mentioned the conference again.

He already knew that Elizabeth's arm was healing almost without any scars at all, that Mr Jacobs was progressing nicely with his artificial larynx and that Minnie and Benjamin had finally chosen a name for their son.

'They've chosen Neil Mark,' Claire announced, lying back on her bed and smiling at the ceiling. 'Neil from my surname and Mark from yours.'

'Really?' Declan was chuffed. 'No one's ever done that for me before.'

'It's a nice feeling,' she agreed.

'How many other children have you had named after you?' he asked, remembering how she'd often delivered babies.

'Two, but this is the first boy.'

'Two? Wow.'

'Yep. Two little Claires running around, although one family moved to Townsville, but they still send me a Christmas card with a photograph every year.'

'Wow. You're my hero. That's a goal I think I'd like to achieve. To have someone call their son Declan after me.'

'Then you'd better change your speciality.' Claire laughed, loving the way he made her feel.

Declan listened to her laughter, knowing she would never leave Mt Black. Not only was her entire family there but it was part of who she was. She loved the people, had been there for them through so many good times and bad. The people, in turn, had been there to support her all those years ago, had helped her hold her family together, and she would never think of leaving.

That therefore meant he would have to open a practice in Mt

Black. He'd studied the demographics of the area and surrounding townships, hoping he could sustain a full-time private practice as well as still doing his monthly clinic week at the hospital. He also planned to sit on the hospital board, knowing they couldn't refuse someone with his qualifications and expertise. That way, things would start to change and start happening in Mt Black Hospital, beginning with appreciating the work performed by their full-time GP.

He was a man with a mission. He was in love with Claire and he intended to marry her. He'd sorted out what he was going to do professionally, not only in Mt Black but Brisbane as well, and now all he needed to do was to convince Claire to marry him.

'Easy,' he said, although his voice didn't sound too confident.

On Wednesday night, Claire disconnected the call, feeling very disconnected and discontented with herself. She usually felt like this after speaking to Declan, but tonight it was worse. Why did he have to be so far away? Why did this hurt so much? She wanted to be with him yet at the same time she didn't want to lose control over her life. Couldn't she have both? Did she want both? She looked at the receiver she'd just replaced, tears welling in her eyes.

Turning over, she buried her face in her pillow and cried. It was strange. It was out of character but she cried. At the soft tap on her bedroom door, she stopped, lifted her head and quickly grabbed a tissue, sniffing. She didn't want her family to know she was this upset over Declan. She took a calming breath, wondering if Brett needed more help with his homework, and immediately tried to get her mind back into gear.

'It's all right,' Mary said softly as she opened the door. 'It's only me.'

Claire relaxed a little. 'Something wrong?'

'That's my question.' Mary came into the room and shut the door. She walked over to the bed and sat down beside Claire, pointing to the phone. 'How's Declan tonight?'

Claire shrugged. 'He's...Declan.'

'You love him, don't you.' It was a statement.

'Yes.'

'And he knows this?'

'Yes.'

'Wow. That's big. How does he feel about you?'

'The same.'

Mary frowned at her. 'Then what's the problem?'

Claire stood and walked away from the bed. 'Just because we say we love each other, it doesn't make the world fall into place. It's not that simple.'

'Sure it is. Greg told me he loved me, I said the same and we got married and lived happily ever after.'

'That's you. You're not me.'

'No. I'm not. I'm not the big sister who's held this family together. I'm not the one who heaped responsibility after responsibility on her shoulders and soldiered on. I'm the second oldest. I'm the sister who is there for the big sister to lean on. I'm her second in command and I'm there to pick up the slack when she needs it. Well, I'm here to tell you—consider the slack picked up.'

'Meaning?'

'Go to him. Go to Declan. Spend some time with him, away from here, away from us and the hospital and the patients. Just go and be in love and enjoy it.'

'And then?'

'And then talk to him. Figure out how you can make this work.'

'I can't leave Mt Black, Mary. I won't, and it's not right for you or Declan or anyone to ask me to.'

'I understand your feelings. It's that defined sense of responsibility getting in the way again.'

'I love this place. I love the people, the hospital, my patients, my siblings, this house.'

'And could you choose all that and *not* Declan?'

Claire bit her lip. 'Are you saying it's either or?'

'I'm not saying that at all. I'm asking you if you'd be content with all that or could you give it all up for Declan?'

Claire opened her mouth to speak but realised she couldn't answer. Life without Declan? The thought made her heart ache, her breathing increase and total panic rose within her. Life without Declan? No. She couldn't do it. She just couldn't. A tear rolled down her cheek. 'I'd give it up,' she said softly, and then cleared her throat. 'I would. I can't believe it. I'd give it all up for Declan.'

'Atta girl. Now you're there.'

'Where?' Claire clenched her hands together.

'You know. Think about it.'

'I'm with Declan.'

'Exactly. Doesn't matter where you are or where he is, you're connected. It's the way it has to be, Claire. That connection enables you to not only depend on each other but still maintain a balance of independence.'

Claire hiccuped a little, then looked at her sister. 'I don't like being out of control and he makes me feel that way.'

'Yet you'd give up everything you hold dear?'

'In a heartbeat.'

Mary smiled and sighed. 'I hoped this day would come and it has. You're right, Claire. Right to be scared, right to feel as though you're losing control. It's because you're taking a step— a step in faith, a step in love. Marriage is about letting go of your control, of allowing someone else to penetrate your inner sanctum. You not only *share* that special place but you also help each other to *grow*. You need to trust Declan as well as love him.'

'I do.'

'Then you need to show him that. You need to open yourself up completely, lay yourself bare and believe that he would never do anything to hurt you. The walls need to come down, right down, so there are no bricks left for him to smash through. I watched you while he was here and every night the frown lines on your forehead became deeper and deeper.'

'Gee, thanks.'

'But there was also a radiance about you—a glow I've never seen before—and that's why I'm here, sticking my nose in. Let go of the control, Claire. Trust him just like you trust us. Look at what you've accomplished. Your goal was to hold this family together when Mum and Dad died and you've done exactly that.

Lizzie and Jase are working and they're both so happy. Thomas is doing a brilliant job at uni and Brett, well, our little smarty pants will no doubt get Dux of his school. I'm happily married and doing a job I love and you…with all the pressure you've had on your life, you've put yourself through medical school and are now caring for your patients the way you've always cared for us.

'You give and you give and you give. It's time to take because if you don't take, you rob others of the opportunity to be givers. Declan wants to give, too, Claire. You need to let him. You need to trust him. You need to let go of your need to always be in control. Lean on him. Let him be strong for you. There will be surprises, some good, some not so good, but if you're together—whether here or somewhere else—you'll be able to cope simply because you have each other.'

Two more tears trickled down Claire's cheeks. 'I want to. I want to be happy. To be with him.'

'Then do that.'

'But—'

'No. No more buts. Answer this question for me. If Mum and Dad were here today, if they were here to take that parental responsibility from you, what would you do? Would you run to Declan with open arms?'

'Yes.' There was no hesitation.

'Than consider that burden lifted. We're all adults now. Brett may not officially be eighteen years old but that's only a few months away and really, when you look at the official adults out there in the world, most of them don't have as much common sense as he does.'

'That's true.'

'You've done your job, big sister. You've held us together and we're going to stay together, for ever, but right now it's time for you to let go. To go and have your own adventures. To find your centre of happiness and to let that radiate out to the rest of us.'

Claire blew her nose once more and looked at Mary. 'How did you get to be so smart?'

Mary laughed and hugged her sister. 'I've had the best example to follow all my life—even before Mum and Dad died. It was you. You're the best, Claire, and I love you very much.'

Claire hugged her sister back and then took three deep breaths. 'Declan wants me to go to a conference on the Gold Coast.'

'When?'

'Tomorrow night. The conference is Friday, Saturday and Sunday—as if you didn't know. He told me he'd spoken to you.'

'Did he now?'

'Well, not in so many words.'

'And does that bother you?'

Claire thought for a moment and then shook her head. 'No.'

'You're going, right?'

'Well…' Claire shrugged. If she didn't, she'd be letting her fear, her fear of letting go of control, win. She not only owed it to herself and her siblings to go but she owed it to Declan. He loved her. He'd said it over and over again. He wasn't trying to run her life, take away her independence or interfere. He wanted to help her grow, to help her excel at something she was good at, to help her be everything she could be.

So what if he'd organised things. Wasn't that a nice surprise? Wasn't that exactly what she would do for someone else? She'd helped all her siblings, she'd helped her patients. It was a nice gesture and she should accept it and be happy. Let someone give to her for a change.

Claire nodded. 'I'm going.' The words were said softly, then she cleared her throat and said with more conviction, 'I'm going.'

'Atta girl.'

'I'm going to go and see Declan and we're going to work this out.'

'That's what I want to hear.'

Claire giggled. 'You sound like a football coach.'

'I feel like one.' Mary looked closely at her. 'But this is good, right?'

'Yes. This is good *and* it's right. Declan's the guy for me.'

CHAPTER ELEVEN

DECLAN stood at the airport, a bouquet in his arms, hoping Claire had pushed passed her stubbornness and had got on the plane. The flight from Mt Black had landed and he was now waiting impatiently to see if she disembarked.

What if she didn't come? What if she hadn't chosen to spend time with him? Doubts had racked him last night and he'd thought they might have disappeared with the morning light but no. Claire was the only one who could dispel his doubts. The time he'd spent apart from her had been so difficult. Absence had made the heart grow fonder, as well as totally impatient. His love had grown, yes, but he'd all but forced her to come. It was important, though. Couldn't she see that? They needed to spend more time together, to get to know each other on a deeper level. They needed to sort out their future. He needed her, with every breath he dragged into his lungs—he needed her.

He watched carefully as a few people came through the doors. He didn't recognise any of them. Business people, returning from trips. Was she there? Had she come? He held his breath.

Then he saw her and his heart felt as though it would break through his rib cage it pounded so hard. He breathed in, drinking in the sight of her, unable to believe she was really that beautiful.

His Claire. She was here. She'd come!

He waited impatiently for the rest of the people to clear before he made his way to her. His smile was wide and ecstatic as he walked directly up to her. 'Claire.' He reached for her hand and the instant they touched, the chemistry that had flowed between them since they'd first met surged stronger and harder through them both.

Claire was cross with him. Wasn't she? She was still a bit annoyed he'd organised her the way he had but now she was here, looking at him, touching him, all her previous feelings melted away, leaving only her heart filled with love.

He was here. They were together. She had to have confidence they could work everything out. She needed to believe there would be happily ever after for both of them. She loved him so much, she wasn't going to have it any other way.

Declan swallowed, still stunned by her beauty. Her eyes were so deep, so brown, so mesmerising. And her hair... She'd left it loose and he let go of her hand to tenderly trail his fingers through the blonde tresses. 'How was the flight?' His voice was deep and husky, filled with repressed desire.

'Well...' she whispered. 'Um...' Her gaze locked with his and she breathed in deeply, loving the spicy scent of him as it wound itself about her.

'Ah...I know that cue.' He smiled and bent his head to trail kisses across her cheek. Claire closed her eyes at the feel of his lips against her skin. How had she lived so long without his touch? It was a miracle both of them had survived.

'Now, wasn't "um" the part where I nuzzle your neck?' he whispered tantalizingly, and Claire felt her knees go weak.

She leaned into him and one arm came about her, instantly supporting her. 'Who cares?' she whispered back. 'Just hurry up and kiss me.'

'Mmm.' Without another word his mouth found hers and both drank hungrily from the oasis. It had been far too long and in that one moment Declan promised himself it would never be that long again. Here was the woman he loved, soft and perfect in his arms, and he never wanted it to be any other way again.

A few people passed them, sighing at the sight they made. Someone else jostled them and they broke apart. Claire glanced around, amazed she'd made such a public spectacle of herself but when she looked back into Declan's eyes, those inhibitions fled.

'You are so perfect for me,' he murmured, and Claire nodded.

He held her gaze for a moment longer, then said, 'We'd better go,' his voice deep and husky. Keeping his arm around her, he breathed in her scent, marvelling at the fact that she was really here, in his arms, looking up at him with love in her eyes. He found it hard to think logically but knew if he wanted to get her somewhere a little more private, he needed to allow logic to intrude. 'Any bags?'

'No.' She patted her shoulder-bag. 'Just this.'

'Great.' It was then he remembered the bouquet in his hand. 'Oops. I almost forgot.' He held out his offering and Claire immediately broke into laughter.

'Declan. They're...beautiful.' She glanced down at the Cellophane-wrapped bunch of paintbrushes and mixing spatulas.

'The paints and canvas are back home. I couldn't figure out how to wrap them properly.' He took her shoulder-bag from her before putting his arm about her. 'Let's go.' He walked her out to his car and stowed her bag in the back.

'At home?' Claire asked after he'd navigated the traffic out of the airport. 'I thought I was staying in a hotel?'

'I never said that.'

'Yes, you did.'

'No. I said your accommodation was taken care of. My parents have a big house.'

'Declan!'

'I know. You don't like surprises. That's why I'm telling you now instead of when I pull up in their driveway.'

'I don't want to impose.'

'No imposition. Besides, I've met your family. It's only fair you meet mine.'

Claire remembered Mary's words and nodded, knowing she needed to trust him. 'You don't feel...anxious about that?'

'About introducing you to them? No.' He shook his head for emphasis. 'I love you, I love them. I know you'll get along perfectly with my parents and my siblings.'

'You're that sure?'

'Yes.' He stopped at a red light and smiled at her. 'I've got nothing to be anxious about.' He quickly leaned over and brushed a kiss across her lips. 'You give me confidence, Claire, and with that confidence comes a decrease in the anxiety. See how perfect you are for me?'

'Er…yes.'

The light turned green and he started to drive once more. Claire also realised there were other green lights flashing all around her and total happiness swelled in her heart. Had she ever dreamt of feeling this way? So happy and so content? Perhaps, long ago, as a child when both her parents had been alive. Now those emotions blended with the love and trust that already coursed through her. He was here. Declan was here! He was holding her close and she could touch him, feel him, kiss him, and that was all she'd been wanting since he'd walked away from her nearly three weeks ago.

For most of the drive to his parents' house he held her hand as they talked of general things, Declan pointing out some of the sights and Claire marvelling at the plethora of high-rise buildings that seemed to line the coast.

'First time here?'

'Yes.'

'Then you're going to love it.'

'Hang on. How am I going to love it and why do I have painting supplies at your parents' house? I thought I was here for a conference.'

'You are.'

'Then aren't I going to be busy listening to specialists talk and learning how to be a refreshed GP?'

'Yes, but you do get time off, Claire. The schedule begins at ten each morning and finishes at four.'

'That's not long.'

'That's what most conferences are like on the Gold Coast. People don't only come here to sit in stuffy conference rooms. They come here to enjoy the sun, the sand and the surf…and the theme parks.'

'I don't surf.'

'No. You paint. I want you to relax. To enjoy yourself. You may be here for the conference but you're also here for you.'

'And for you,' she pointed out.

He pulled up in his parents' driveway and cut the engine.

'And for me.' He undid his seat belt then turned to face her. 'I couldn't wait any longer to see you, Claire. I need you.'

'I need you, too,' she murmured, and found her mouth once more captured with his.

'There's a lot we need to discuss,' he murmured between the frantic kisses they shared.

'I know.'

He pulled back a little and gazed down into her eyes. 'I've tried to give you time and space but I couldn't.'

Claire placed her fingers across his lips. 'Shh. We'll talk. We'll sort everything out but right now I need you to kiss me again.'

A slow smile touched his lips. 'As you wish, Doctor.' Declan's mouth found hers with the sense of being welcomed home and he loved that sensation. He'd never felt this way before and he knew what he shared with Claire would definitely last a lifetime. She'd said they'd sort everything out. That was good, right? That meant she was willing to listen, to compromise, to let go of the control she'd held onto so tightly. Right?

Declan forced all thoughts from his mind and concentrated on kissing her. It was what he'd wanted for so long, to have Claire back in his arms, his mouth on hers. Now she was here and he could touch her as much as he needed to, to kiss her, to lose himself in her.

'Whoo-hoo!' a male teenage voice called. 'Way to go, Dec!'

At the sound of his siblings outside the car, Declan immediately broke off and glared around at them. Evan was knocking on the driver's side window and grinning, his braces showing. Claire started to laugh as she realised they were surrounded—a twin on either side.

Declan felt his annoyance drain at Claire's response. 'Remember teenagers?'

'All too well,' Claire replied, and Declan realised she understood perfectly. 'Let's go.' Claire gathered up her 'bouquet' and climbed from the car, smiling at the teenage girl. 'Hi. I'm Claire.' She held out her free hand and noticed the girl hesitate for a split second.

'I'm Helen.'

'Nice to meet you.' Claire took in the beautiful features of the girl before her, knowing she'd be breaking a lot of hearts when she got older.

'Sorry about Evan,' Helen said, disgusted with her brother. 'He's such a *boy*.'

Claire's smile increased. 'I know all about them. I have three younger brothers.'

'Oh, wow, and I thought Evan was bad enough. He's a real pain. Declan's great, you know, because he's so much older, but some days I could do without Ev being in my face. Do you have any sisters?'

'Two.'

'Wow. That's a lot of kids. I've always wanted a sister but Mum and I are really good friends so I guess that's like having a sister in a way.'

Declan collected Claire's bag. 'Let's go inside.' He put his arm about her waist as they headed in. The twins barrelled in behind them, Evan pushing his way in front of his sister.

'Hi. I'm Evan.' He held out his hand and Claire shook it, smiling at him. Where Helen had been more reserved, more like Declan, Evan seemed the total opposite. He bounced and laughed and was as bright as the sun.

'Pleased to meet you.'

'Declan says he's in love with you. Do you love him back?'

'Evan!' The word came from the doorway and Claire looked up to find a stunning woman standing there and could immediately see where Helen had inherited her looks. She had long jet-black hair and blue eyes. She looked not much older than Declan but Claire instantly knew, more from the tone in her voice when she'd said Evan's name, that this was Declan's mother. 'I'm so sorry,' she said, and made way for them all to enter. 'Evan, go unload the dishwasher, please.'

'Aw, Mum.'

'Evan!'

'All right. All right. I'm going.'

'Helen? Can you get the washing in, please?'

'Sure, Mum.' Helen headed off.

The woman shook her head and held out both her hands and

to Claire's surprise enveloped her in a hug. 'Welcome, Claire. I'm Rachael. Come in, come in.' She led them into the sitting room. 'I'm so pleased to meet you at last. Declan's told us so much about you.'

'Oh?' Claire turned to look at the man in question but he merely shrugged and she could see quite clearly that his anxiety had indeed gone. He was so confident, so self-assured and he'd said that *she* was the one who'd given him that confidence. Her heart swelled with love.

'I'll just take your bag through to your room.' He held out his hand for her bouquet. 'Want me to take that, too?'

'Yes. Thanks.' She watched him go and turned to face his mother. Usually, Claire would feel worried right about now, being in a new place, a new situation, a place where she had no control—and being left alone with her boyfriend's mother—but she didn't. It was as though Declan's confidence had rubbed off on her and, besides, everything felt so right.

'So I take it the flight was all right?' Rachael asked as they sat down.

'Yes. Fine.'

'Was it difficult, leaving your siblings?'

Claire smiled. 'A little bit. For me at any rate. The rest of them were practically shoving me on the plane, begging me to go have some fun.'

Rachael chuckled. 'Sounds wonderful. Would you like a drink?'

Claire nodded and Rachael went to stand.

'Don't get up. I'll get it,' a male voice said, and Claire turned, expecting to see Declan. Instead she saw a man, older than Declan but almost his twin. He leaned forward and offered his hand. 'I'm Joe.'

If Claire had wanted a glimpse into her future, to see how Declan would age, she now had her answer. Joe was as tall as his son, had the same blue eyes and dark hair but his had more grey at the temples.

Rachael laughed. 'It's a bit daunting, isn't it? They're so much alike.'

'Although I have to say Evan's more like me in personality.'

Joe shrugged and pointed to his hair. 'He's also responsible for most of these grey hairs.'

Declan came back into the room and crossed instantly to Claire's side and sat beside her, taking her hand in his.

'I was just getting drinks,' Joe said. 'Dec?'

'Tea would be great.'

'Claire?'

'Same.' Joe left and a moment later the sound of a loud crash came from the kitchen. Rachael grimaced.

'Evan and Joe, in the kitchen alone.' She stood and shook her head. 'Not a good recipe. Excuse me.'

Left alone, Declan turned to Claire. 'You all right?'

Claire met his gaze, a slow, happy smile on her lips. 'Never better. You?'

'Amazed you're actually here and I can do this.' He pulled her closer, wrapped his arms around her and pressed his lips to hers.

That was the first of many special moments, snapshot moments, they shared that weekend, Claire thought as she came out of the last lecture. The conference had been amazing and just what she'd needed to recharge her professional batteries. She'd been able to totally unwind and for the first time ever she felt free, and it was all thanks to Declan.

His family had been wonderful, including her in their conversations, making her feel welcome. On Saturday, straight after the conference, Declan had picked her up and driven them to the beach where he'd set up her painting supplies and had simply sat on the beach, watching her paint. They'd shared a picnic as the sun had set and Claire had found it very romantic.

Now, on Sunday afternoon, Declan came over and immediately put his arm about her waist, drawing her close. 'How did it go this afternoon?'

'Terrific. *You* were terrific. Great lecture. Everyone was impressed. *I* was impressed.'

'Really?' He smiled and waggled his eyebrows up and down. 'Impressed impressed? Or just impressed?'

Claire laughed. 'Impressed.' She placed her hand on his cheek. 'You're a smart man, Declan. People may or may not understand your brilliance but always know I not only appreciate it, I appreciate *you*. I accept you for the man you are, deep down inside—brains and all.'

Declan drew in a breath and looked down at her with love and admiration. 'That means more to me than any academic accolade.' He brushed his lips across hers. 'We need to go or we'll be late.'

'Late?' She let him rush her through the throng of conference attendees and out to his car. 'Where are we going?'

Declan opened the car door and met her gaze. 'It's a surprise.' He paused. 'Ready to be surprised?'

Claire gazed at him, amazed he knew her so well, so completely. She trusted him. She loved him. 'Yes.'

'Good.'

'Can you tell me where we're going?'

'To the movie set.'

'Where your dad works?'

'Yes.'

'Why? Does he need medical help?'

'Not really. You know the movie set is attached to one of the theme parks?'

'Yes. Evan was telling me. He's very excited his dad gets to meet so many movie stars and stuntmen.'

Declan laughed. 'He's going to turn my mother grey.'

'Why? Because he wants to be a stunt guy?'

'Yes. Anyway, I thought it was something you'd like to see so Dad's arranged for you to have a quick tour of the set. Afterwards we can catch the dusk parade they have every day at the theme park.' He shrugged. 'It's kind of fun.'

'How many times have you seen it?'

'Several hundred. They change it every now and then, depending on what new movies have come out, but the usual superheroes are always there. One of them comes hurtling down the entire length of the street, suspended on a cable above everyone's heads.'

'Just like a super-hero flying away after saving the damsel in distress?'

Declan smiled. 'Exactly. Been watching cartoons?'

'Not lately.' Claire sighed, unable to believe she was so happy.

When they arrived at the theme park, Declan was greeted by the staff like an old friend. 'Been coming here long?' Claire asked.

'Since I first met my dad when I was fourteen.'

'The day you went bungee-jumping?'

'Yeah. It was awesome.'

Claire faltered in her step. 'That's not the surprise, is it?'

Declan laughed and shook his head. 'No. Trust me, Claire.'

'Yes.' She forced herself to let go and relax as they headed onto the movie set. Cameras, cables and crew were everywhere.

'Looks like it's reset time,' Declan murmured. 'They need to reset the scene after every take so they can do it again and again.'

'Being a movie star isn't as glamorous as people think?'

'It's not all sunglasses and autographs.'

To Claire's surprise, not only was Joe on the set but Rachael and the twins as well. 'We sometimes come down for the theme park parade,' Rachael told her, after giving her a hug. Again Claire was astounded at how open and welcoming Declan's family were, Rachael especially. 'How were the lectures today?'

'Fantastic.' Claire watched as Declan spoke to his father. 'Declan was amazing. He's so clear and concise when he explains things, and I was so impressed with him.'

'I'm impressed, too,' Rachael said. 'With you.'

Claire was taken aback at the comment. 'With me?'

'You're good for him, Claire. I've been hoping for so long that Declan would find the perfect woman, a woman who understood his anxiety, who would help him through things, and you're certainly that woman.'

Claire laughed self-consciously. 'I can see where he gets his honesty from.'

'I mean it, Claire. Usually, before he has to give a lecture he doesn't sleep, he doesn't eat. He winds himself up into knots and puts so much extra pressure on himself it's a wonder he can still stand up and think coherently. That didn't happen this time. He's been so relaxed, so at peace. As a mother, it's wonderful to see.'

'I'm sure it's just Declan.'

'No, Claire. It's you. You're the one who's made the difference in his life. He draws strength and confidence from you, and you let him. That's a difficult thing for one person to do for another but you do it.'

Claire shrugged. 'I love him.'

'I know, but it's not just that. It's your gift, Claire. You have the gift of bringing out the best in people and from what Declan's told me, you've done that with your siblings.' Rachael placed her hand on Claire's cheek and said softly, 'Your parents would have been so proud of you.'

Tears welled instantly in Claire's eyes and rolled down her cheeks. She found herself enveloped in Rachael's arms in such a loving and maternal way she felt her body well up with repressed need—the need to have that maternal love. Until that moment, Claire hadn't realised how much she'd missed it.

'Mum? Claire?' Declan said softly. 'Is everything all right?'

Claire pulled back and sniffed, smiling up at him. 'Everything's perfect.'

'The parade's going to start soon,' he said, putting his arms protectively around her.

'Go across, dear. We'll be there soon,' Rachael said.

Declan and Claire walked back to the general theme park section and joined the throng of people lining up for the dusk parade. 'You sure everything's all right?' he asked, looking at her with concern.

'Yes.' She smiled. 'You're family are so…accepting, Declan. Your mother and father… I can see why you hold them in such high esteem. They're amazing.'

'They love you,' he said simply.

'I can feel that and I haven't had that kind of parental love in such a long time.' She hugged him close, feeling the tears threaten once more. 'Thank you for sharing your family with me.'

'That's how I feel about your family. The rowdiness, the sibling rivalry, the fun and laughter. I get that with Helen and Evan, but with your family it's more encompassing for me because they're all closer to my age.' He paused. 'See how perfect we are for each other.'

Claire hugged him close, drinking in the feel, the scent, the need of him.

They continued to wait for the parade and once Claire thought she caught a glimpse of someone who looked like Thomas in the crowd. She shook her head. She was seeing things. Soon the rest of Declan's family joined them and not long after that the parade finally started. There was an announcer, describing the floats and characters as they came down the street, the music loud and lively. Claire watched everything, drinking it in and enjoying herself.

When the parade had gone all the way down the street, the floats now spaced out all the way along, the announcer's voice sounded again.

'And now we have a special presentation for everyone here tonight. Superwoman is going to choose a member from our audience.'

The actress playing Superwoman jumped down from her float and headed into the crowd. Claire smiled, watching eagerly to see who she chose. Her eyes widened when Superwoman came to stand directly in front of her and then took her hand.

'No. It's fine,' Claire said. 'Choose someone else.'

Superwoman didn't say a word but shook her head and led Claire out into the street. Everyone clapped and Claire looked back at Declan, concerned. He smiled encouragingly and winked at her. It was then Claire realised that *this* was part of her surprise.

She looked around at the crowd who were all clapping and cheering, and this time she didn't just think she saw Thomas— she *did* see him. And not only him. Mary and Greg, Elizabeth and Jason and Brett, too. They were all there. Standing with the crowd, watching her and smiling.

Claire glanced back at Declan, her eyes wide with concern. What was going on? Why were her family here? He winked at her again and she finally remembered to breathe.

Trust him. Just trust him. You love him. He loves you. Just trust him. The words kept repeating over and over in her head and once Superwoman had taken Claire back to the float and helped her to climb up, the announcer's voice came again, although this time it wasn't the same voice. It was a more familiar voice and she realised it was Declan's.

Holding a microphone, he walked towards her, looking at her standing up on the float. 'Claire Neilson, you have been chosen. You are an amazing woman, a caring, giving woman. A doctor who's given so much of her time and her life to other people. *My* Superwoman. The woman—the *only* woman—I will ever love.'

At his words, a cheer went up from the audience around them. Claire swallowed but didn't care about them. She only had eyes for Declan. Slowly he climbed up onto the float, still talking.

'You are perfect for me. You give me confidence…confidence to make a public fool of myself because I am a fool in love… with you.' As he said the last two words, he came to stand in front of her and dropped to one knee.

Superwoman took the microphone from him and Claire watched as Declan withdrew something from his pocket. It was a ring, she realised. A diamond ring. He cleared his throat and Superwoman held the microphone to his mouth.

'Claire—please, be my wife.'

Again the crowd went wild but Claire didn't care. She looked down at her siblings who were nodding their heads eagerly, Brett clapping, Thomas whistling. She looked across at Declan's family, all standing together, Joe and Rachael with their arms around each other, and then she looked back at Declan. *Her* Declan. Nothing mattered, except the two of them. She gazed down into his eyes and nodded.

'Remember when you told me how when you'd first met your dad you felt as though you'd found the missing piece? You didn't realise a piece was missing until then? Well, that's how I feel, Declan. I didn't realise a piece of me was missing until you turned up. Now, with you by my side, I'm complete. You complete me, Declan. I love you.' She held out her hand and he placed the ring on her finger before she tugged him up and wrapped her arms around him. The loud music started again and everyone clapped and cheered, but for Claire it was just the two of them.

'I know you can't leave Mt Black, Claire. I know that and I'd never ask you to.'

'I want to be with you. I don't care where.'

'Good, because do you really think after making such a public spectacle of ourselves I'm going to let you go? Change has never been easy for me but with you by my side I feel as though I can accomplish anything. I want to move to Mt Black, Claire. I can still do the clinic at the hospital as well as opening a private practice.'

'But your job? In Brisbane?'

'I've never settled there. You know that. Now I know why. I wasn't supposed to be there in the first place.'

'Change is difficult for you. Letting go of control is difficult for me.'

'But together we can do it.'

'Yes.' She nodded. 'Together, we can do it.' She pressed her mouth to his and felt the truth of those words.

There was a loud bang and they both looked up. Another super-hero was hurtling on the cable towards them, flying overhead, and when he passed their location a flood of confetti came raining down on them.

Claire laughed and shook her head. 'Oh, Declan, when you let go of your anxiety, you let go big time.'

'I wanted to show you how much you mean to me, how much I love you. I wanted to shout it to the world.'

'You have...and you did the most perfect job.'

MILLS & BOON®

0806/03b

Live the emotion

MedicaL
romance™

RESCUED BY MARRIAGE by *Dianne Drake*

Dr Della Riordan is in need of some luck – she really needs to get her life back on track! The practice on Redcliffe Island seems too good to be true; with gorgeous Dr Sam Montgomery on hand to help, Della begins to find her feet... But Sam is hiding a secret that could well bring an end to Della's dreams.

THE NURSE'S LONGED-FOR FAMILY
by *Fiona Lowe*

Jess Henderson is balancing her nursing job with being mother to Woody, her two-year-old nephew. Gorgeous Dr Alex Fitzwilliam manages to convince her that there is always time for romance... But Alex refuses to confront his feelings over the loss of his own son. Alex must put his feelings aside if they have any chance of becoming a family.

HER BABY'S SECRET FATHER
by *Lynne Marshall*

When Nurse Jaynie Winchester goes into premature labour, no-one comes rushing to her side. Baby Tara is delivered, and Jaynie is not the only one willing the tiny mite to survive. Respiratory therapist Terrance Zanderson finds himself getting involved with this family, then Terrance realises who Tara's father is...

On sale 1st September 2006

Available at WHSmith, Tesco, ASDA, Borders, Eason, Sainsbury's and most bookshops

www.millsandboon.co.uk

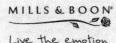

"I was fifteen when my mother finally told me the truth about my father. She didn't mean to. She meant to keep it a secret forever. If she'd succeeded it might have saved us all."

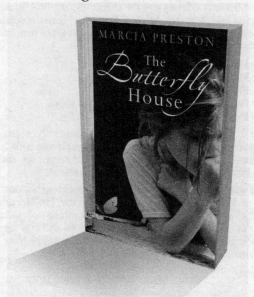

When a hauntingly familiar stranger knocks on Roberta Dutreau's door, she is compelled to begin a journey of self-discovery leading back to her childhood. But is she ready to know the truth about what happened to her, her best friend Cynthia and their mothers that tragic night ten years ago?

16th June 2006

MIRA

FREE

4 BOOKS AND A SURPRISE GIFT!

We would like to take this opportunity to thank you for reading this Mills & Boon® book by offering you the chance to take FOUR more specially selected titles from the Medical Romance™ series absolutely FREE! We're also making this offer to introduce you to the benefits of the Mills & Boon® Reader Service™—

> ★ FREE home delivery
> ★ FREE gifts and competitions
> ★ FREE monthly Newsletter
> ★ Books available before they're in the shops
> ★ Exclusive Reader Service offers

Accepting these FREE books and gift places you under no obligation to buy; you may cancel at any time, even after receiving your free shipment. Simply complete your details below and return the entire page to the address below. You don't even need a stamp!

YES! Please send me 4 free Medical Romance books and a surprise gift. I understand that unless you hear from me, I will receive 6 superb new titles every month for just £2.80 each, postage and packing free. I am under no obligation to purchase any books and may cancel my subscription at any time. The free books and gift will be mine to keep in any case.

M6ZEE

Ms/Mrs/Miss/Mr...Initials ....
BLOCK CAPITALS PLEASE

Surname ....

Address ....

....

....Postcode ....

Send this whole page to:
The Reader Service, FREEPOST CN81, Croydon, CR9 3WZ